ULTIMATE UNOFFICIAL MINECRAFT CHALLENGE

A Collection of Creative, Collaborative
Projects That Connect In-Game
Challenges with Hands-on Activities

John Miller and Chris Fornell Scott

QUARRY

Contents

Introduction

In an age where games have multimillion-dollar budgets, high-end computer graphics, and Hollywood-inspired storylines, how can a game that comes with no instructions, no clear goals, and no-frills blocky graphics become a mega-hit widely lauded for its creative and immersive play?

Perhaps it's because players walk away from a Minecraft session with a deep sense of fulfillment and are highly motivated to return and improve their skills. Minecraft challenges them to explore a new, unlimited world and interact with other players and the environment. They mine for resources and craft tools that they use to modify their environment to fit their needs. Or perhaps it's because Minecraft is versatile and highly adaptable to any player at any experience level and has something to teach everyone. Its open-ended nature provides rich opportunities for exploration and discovery and satisfies a natural inquisitiveness while promoting detailed and deep conversations, both in and out of the game.

Adults might assume that playing Minecraft is just like playing any other video game, but kids know that Minecraft offers much more than entertainment. As kids become experts in Minecraft, they create a knowledge gap that is often difficult for adults to bridge. Players can speak the language of Minecraft while nonplayers may be confused.

This book bridges that gap. It's designed for adults who want to connect with their Minecraft players by improving their understanding of the game and by extending their child's learning with both in- and out-of-game activities. It also connects STEM—concepts in science, technology, engineering, and math—with Minecraft play. Additionally, the book employs analog (community) connections that encourage kids to interact with the adults in their lives. New conversations and paths of creativity will reveal themselves as you complete both the in-game and out-of-game portions of the individual labs and the quests (a set of four labs). In some instances, you'll help the Minecraft expert with the analog connections, and at other times, the game expert will teach you how to build in-game portions of the lab.

What Can Minecraft Teach?

You only need to peek just beneath the surface of Minecraft to uncover rich and varied learning experiences. Minecraft encourages players to create, share, and innovate as no other game has ever done before. It promotes continuous learning. Teaching and learning from others is as much a part of the game as building a shelter or fighting creepers. While playing in creative mode, with an unlimited supply of every block in their inventory available, players have the freedom to explore their imagination. Players monitor their inventories, conduct ongoing needs assessments, and consider options to expand and improve their character's status in the game. By learning more skills and discovering or crafting more resources, players better prepare themselves for each day, and the reward for their hard work is enhanced playability. When playing in survival mode, players must rely upon a varied and changing set of skills to achieve their immediate and long-term goals.

Minecraft encourages numerous positive traits and builds life skills and spatial understanding. Players develop problem-solving strategies for surviving each night while setting and prioritizing goals for the next day. Food is important, but so is shelter. Armor and weapons will help fight off mobs but require specific and often hard-to-find resources and crafting. It is only through perseverance and planning that players will be successful.

Further, players value the craftsmanship and skills of others while sharing knowledge and innovations, especially in creative multiplayer mode. They develop large-scale, imaginative, team-oriented projects and break down tasks to assign pieces to players based on skill sets. This interdependence builds positive relationships and flexible thinkers.

The vast amount of creative and humorous storytelling and adventure sharing online reflects Minecraft's popularity. Thousands of websites and YouTube videos are dedicated to design tutorials, building, and gameplay strategies. Survival tips, creative ideas, and answers to player questions are only a click or two away on the Internet. Younger players follow and often imitate their favorite YouTube stars, producing and sharing videos and tutorials of their own and emulating a business model for the twenty-first century.

MINECRAFT IN SCHOOLS

Educators are using Minecraft as a tool for learning in most grade levels and content areas in classrooms around the world, and have discovered that their students remain engaged, highly motivated, and excited to share their expertise while demonstrating their learning as they use a favorite game.

The game's encouragement of sharing ideas and seeking help via a thriving and popular Facebook group (*facebook.com/playcraftlearn*) energizes educators as well. Some teachers create and share Minecraft worlds and the associated lesson plans that target specific concepts, skills, and units of study. Some worlds come complete with buildings and nonplayer characters ready for students to explore and interact with. Other teachers design worlds for focused student or team collaboration and task students with building out the world to meet content objectives. Educators are also connecting classrooms globally through large-scale team builds and exploration, with multiple schools learning in a single world designed by a team of teachers.

The scale of every block in Minecraft represents 1 cubic meter, so applications in mathematics and geometry are clear. Students can visualize concepts such as area, perimeter, and volume

Command blocks automate in-game processes like teleportation, item sharing, and gameplay conditions, which leaves the teacher more time for working with students.

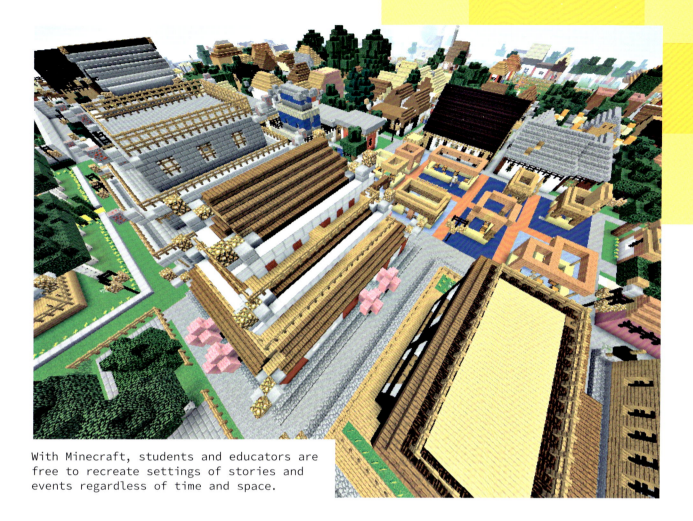

With Minecraft, students and educators are free to recreate settings of stories and events regardless of time and space.

in three dimensions. Students can demonstrate ratio, proportion, and fractions using Minecraft, as well as collect and graph data, all in the game world. Science teachers have discovered they can use Minecraft to teach geology, physics, and biology. Students are aptly creating models of plate tectonics, DNA, animal cells, and even quantum behavior. Redstone blocks in Minecraft release a power source that students and teachers can use to explore electrical circuitry and operate switches, pistons, and logic gates. Students are able to learn and apply computer code within the game and explore rich and diverse ocean biomes.

Minecraft is also great for teaching social sciences and literacy. Students demonstrate their understanding of setting, plot, theme, and conflict by recreating children's stories and young adult novels scene by scene. Books and journals within the game can support student- and teacher-generated text and can include live links to information available on the Internet.

Historical figures can come alive in Minecraft and interact with students in ways traditional textbooks cannot. By role-playing with characters from history, students can experience the wonders of ancient Greece or explore a Civil War battlefield with a virtual soldier and then reflect on their adventures through journal writing and interactions with each other.

You can find a wealth of resources for using Minecraft for teaching and learning at education. minecraft.net.

How To Use This Book

Each of the four labs within the six quests has both an in-game and an out-of-game activity, which is called the "family activity." Most labs suggest doing the out-of-game activities first as a way to research and prepare for in-game building. Flip through the quests to get a feel for the flow of the book.

You can either work through the labs sequentially, or you can bounce from one lab to another. If you're new to Minecraft, consider starting at the beginning, as Quest 1 introduces basic gameplay. You can also use the labs to connect your child's love of the game with an out-of-game learning experience. For example, if you're planning to visit a museum, consider skipping to Lab 11, Creating Figures, which is a perfect fit for that experience. You can also use the labs to connect your child's love of the game with an out-of-game learning experience.

Use this book as a bridge between Minecraft players (usually kids) and their nonplayer counterparts (typically parents or teachers). Sit down with your children and pick a place to start. We want this book to open and build communication, collaboration, creativity, and critical thinking between kids and adults. Nonplayers will learn about Minecraft, while players will enjoy learning about analog, community, and other out-of-game connections.

We encourage you to start building in Minecraft with your kids to further develop your bond. Minecraft is an immersive experience that naturally offers opportunities to try, fail, and try again. Use those same principles as you work with your Minecraft player on the out-of-game part of each lab.

MINECRAFT BASICS

WHAT IS MINECRAFT?

Minecraft is a game. Yet, since its inception in 2009, it has evolved into an amazing tool for creating, innovating, teaching, and learning. It absorbs players in a blocky, three-dimensional world where they are free to explore and create whatever they can think of using a simple interface. With over 300 million copies sold, it has become one of the world's all-time best-selling games.

Minecraft is a unique game in that there are no levels that you pass to continue on inside the game. The game is open-ended, where you create the experience for yourself as you play. The basics of playing Minecraft encourage collaboration and not competition. Certainly players can turn the game into a competitive experience, by playing player versus player (PvP) or racing through a parkour map. When playing in "survival" mode, players gain experience (XP) in a variety of skills.

SINGLE PLAYER VS. MULTIPLAYER

You can play Minecraft alone or with others; and there's no difference in the in-game mechanics between the two. Purchasing a Minecraft account allows players to play in either mode, but it also depends on the platform. All players must have their own license and, generally, their own copy of the game for the platform they are using. Some exceptions include console editions.

Playing in single player mode is a solitary yet interactive experience commonly used by players to hone their skills or develop worlds or maps without the potential for interruption from others.

Individuals can open or otherwise share their worlds at any time with other players.

In multiplayer mode, players interact with each other, oftentimes collaborating to achieve common goals and develop strategies for expansion and resource accumulation. Through cooperative play and experimentation, players polish their skills in areas like redstone mining, building, and food production. Compared to most other games, Minecraft removes the arguing often associated with playing collaboratively.

CREATIVE MODE AND SURVIVAL MODE

Players must decide between two common game mode options when beginning a new game: creative mode and survival mode. (You may hear players talk about a third option for play known as adventure mode. This mode preserves structures and special modifications and limits destructive behaviors or "griefing" from visitors to the map.)

In "creative" mode, every player has access to an unlimited supply of blocks of every kind. They can fly high in the air and dive deep under water without fear of dying. Players cannot harm others or be killed or attacked by mobs; they don't need to eat or worry about their health. They can concentrate instead on creating whatever their minds can think of. When players are playing in this mode with others, builds can reach epic proportions.

When first playing in "survival" mode, players quickly discover that they need to feed themselves and avoid falls from high places to stay healthy. Loss of health due to hunger or physical activity will eventually lead to death. They will also discover that when nighttime comes, they are susceptible to attack by monsters like zombies and creepers.

Players in survival mode begin play with nothing and, through exploration of their environment, gather resources like wood and stone. They then craft these blocks into tools, weapons, and other useful items. They must construct a shelter to keep the monsters out at night and acquire food by killing animals or harvesting seeds and growing crops. As days and nights pass, players become more proficient at gathering resources and crafting items. Weapons and armor protect players from monsters, allowing them to travel at night and explore more of their unique world.

BUILDING BLOCKS
Players in creative mode have unlimited access to all blocks.

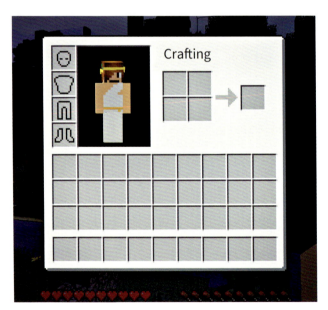

CRAFTING
When you are playing in survival mode, your inventory starts completely empty. Begin by punching trees to collect wood. Each box is ready to store the materials you mine.

SHARING LABS AND QUESTS

Sharing builds is integral to the Minecraft experience. Some players share by inviting others to play in their world; others take screenshots and make videos. This section of the book offers some suggestions on how and where to share Minecraft creations.

YOUTUBE

Want to help your Minecraft-loving counterpart be the next DanTDM or Stacyplays? We've got some quick tips on how to get going. If you have a Google account, you already have a YouTube account. If your Minecraft player is under thirteen, we suggest creating a joint Google account. Use the joint account to upload and share videos.

It's easy to upload your content to share with the Minecraft community. Here are some ways to make a successful video for YouTube:

Edit the video. YouTube has a decent video editor built into the platform. Go to YouTube.com/editor to learn how to clip sections, add music and text, and even annotate the videos with info cards. Info cards are clickable pop-up boxes that allow viewers to subscribe or be redirected to an outside website.

Choose the music. Most music is copyrighted and not free to reuse or add to your video. In the YouTube video editor, you can access free music to add to your videos. Another great place to find free music is the Creative Commons Music site *creativecommons.org/legalmusicforvideos*. Of course, you can always create your own music.

Would you watch it? One of the best benchmarks for good videos is to ask yourself, "Would I watch it?" This simple question is quite powerful. You watched the video as you edited it, but would you watch the video if you didn't know who had created it? If you're not sure, upload your video and make it unlisted. Share your unlisted video with other family and friends to get feedback.

The audience is tough. If you feel like you need to make excuses for your video, redo the video. The audience on YouTube is typically pretty tough on videos that should have been edited better. Watch other videos with a critical eye to learn more.

Video settings. Choose your visibility setting when uploading your videos. YouTube gives three choices: public, unlisted, and private. Public videos are easily searchable by anyone online, unlisted videos are not searchable but can be easily shared with the video link, and private videos can only be viewed by you.

Allow or disallow comments. If you are making videos public and are concerned about negative comments, consider leaving comments off. Under your channel, select the video you've uploaded. You can control whether viewers can leave comments. Go to advanced settings to find the option to turn off comments. It's also possible to review comments before they are posted.

BLOGGING

Start a blog to hold screenshots of your creations as you work through this book. Blogging is a great way to include more learning and exploration as you play and make your creations visible and helpful to others.

The best blogs encourage others to create and think. Both Google Sites and Weebly.com offer a free and easy-to-use blogging platform.

SCREENCASTING

Screencasting is how your favorite YouTubers record their gameplay. The screencasting tool is different for every device you play on. Capture and Share is now built in to the Xbox, Playstation, and Nintendo Switch consoles. There are several free or inexpensive options for screencasting for PC and tablets. Here's a list:

Windows/Mac

+ Camtasia $
+ Adobe Captivate $$$
+ ScreenPal *free*

Tablet

Between the time of writing and publishing this book, there will likely be even more apps available. We suggest doing a search for "screencasting" or "record screen."

SCREENSHOTS

Screenshots are pictures of the device screen. Every device has a way of snapping a picture of what is on the screen. We've listed some examples of how to grab a screenshot below; please note that your device may be different.

+ **PC** Press F2 to grab a screenshot inside the game. Once the screenshot is taken you'll see text in the chat area that lets you know the filename. To find the screenshots on a Windows machine, click on Search and type the word Run. In the new "run" program, type %appdata%, which will reveal hidden folders including .minecraft, which has a screenshots folder. On a Mac, go to Library/Application Support/ minecraft/screenshots.

+ **Tablet** For Apple products, press and hold both the home button and the power button simultaneously. The image is saved in your camera roll. Android varies based on the operating system. Typically, hold the down volume key and the power button at the same time. The screenshot will be saved in the gallery.

+ **Console** For Xbox, double tap the Xbox button, then the Y button. For PlayStation, press and hold the share button for at least one second.

THE MINECRAFT SKILL SET

It should come as no surprise that educators are using Minecraft to support learning across the curriculum and at all grade levels. What might surprise parents and nongamers is how this game has inspired young and old alike to forge careers and reinvent themselves as content producers and creators, designers, professional builders, server managers, and YouTube personalities.

It seems Minecraft has spawned not just a generation of players but also a community of highly creative and innovative practitioners. Everyone who plays this game comes away with a sense of wonder at the experience and generally can't wait to return to dig, build, and craft. But is there actual learning going on while playing this game and does it transfer to real-life skills?

Researchers and educators who have experience with Minecraft often point to a set of complex skills that players experience and encounter while engaging in gameplay. These include:

+ **Analytical skills:** Players see or anticipate a problem and can visualize and articulate it to others. Maybe there is a mob spawner in the next room, and you have to figure out how to shut it down. Or, perhaps, you want to build an automated fireworks show using redstone.

+ **Critical thinking:** Players take the facts they have gathered and make decisions. This is especially important when designing sophisticated mechanisms. Minecraft is a safe place to make mistakes through trial and error and to work through testing a hypothesis.

+ **Problem-solving and creative thinking:** This is the most broadly employable and demanded skill. A day does not go by in Minecraft without players reacting to a problem they face, be it in creatively designing a building or in performing a needs analysis to determine crafting priorities.

+ **Communication:** Communication from the onset of any project is critical, whether it is among peers or between service providers and clients. Multiplayer Minecraft games are immensely popular, and designing and building these massive worlds involves dozens of people, including many specialists. Effective communication strategies are critical throughout the process.

+ **Soft skills:** These refer to character traits that enable us to get along with each other. Players are often asked to be patient, express empathy, and monitor self-control during the game. Cooperative teamwork and a strong work ethic are expected for builds to be successful.

A Final Word

It's our hope that the adults who use this book will have an open mind and be an active participant in each of our labs. You'll share what we've discovered by playing alongside our students and children. Minecraft provides a family-friendly immersive experience. It is collaborative and encourages creative problem-solving and rewards logical thinking, deduction, and patient problem-solving. Effective communication is key to its success. It's a game, but it's also a training ground for the next generation of business leaders, entrepreneurs, scientists, and great thinkers.

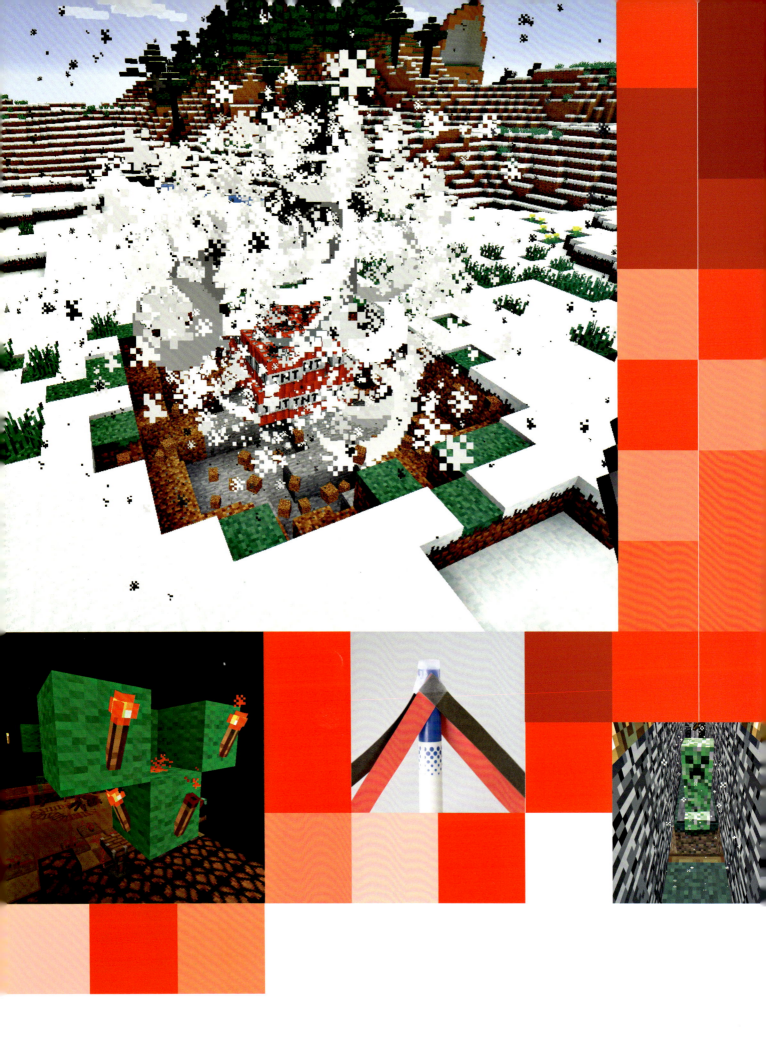

QUEST 1

Using Your Inventory

In this quest, you'll be using all the blocks in your inventory. Start with the basics and strengthen your skills.

Do You Mine?

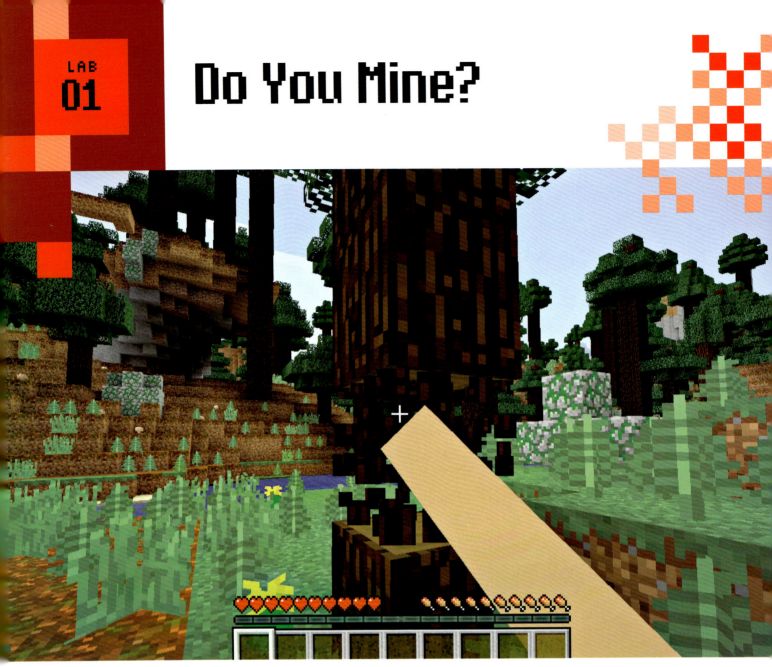

There's no right way to play Minecraft. It's a sandbox game—meaning that it's open-ended rather than structured—where players are free to explore, mine, and craft their experiences.

The act of mining is one of the key activities in Minecraft, and looking for the right blocks, or materials, can sometimes feel like a digital scavenger hunt. In the family activity, you'll hunt for real-life versions of items you'll find inside the game.

Crafting is the second key activity of the game. For the Minecraft part of this lab, you'll use resources you mine to craft useful items to make living and crafting more fun. You'll start at the beginning by punching trees and move toward crafting tools and a shelter, which is how everyone starts playing.

👥 FAMILY ACTIVITY

Scavenger Hunt

A scavenger hunt is a fun way to get your hands dirty while looking for the items on the list. Be sure to work together, as some of the items might be difficult to spot.

⧗ APPROXIMATE TIME TO COMPLETE
45 minutes

✂ MATERIALS
+ Scavenger Hunt Checklist (see page 133 for the complete list)
+ Timer

1. Share the scavenger hunt list on page 133 with your team. Consider how you can work together to tackle the list quickly. This is a time challenge, too!

2. Set the timer for 45 minutes and begin.

3. Once the time is up, add up the number of items you found.

MORE TO EXPLORE

Minecraft was originally called Cave Game. Markus Persson, also known as Notch, started the game with the simple premise of mining to craft. The version you'll play today has more tools, blocks, and resources than any previous version.

Scavenger Hunt Checklist

- ☐ Apple
- ☐ Bed
- ☐ Boat
- ☐ Bow and arrow
- ☐ Bread
- ☐ Cactus
- ☐ Cake
- ☐ Carpet
- ☐ Carrot
- ☐ Clay
- ☐ Coal or charcoal
- ☐ Cobweb
- ☐ Compass

- ☐ Flower pot
- ☐ Flowers
- ☐ Furnace
- ☐ Glass
- ☐ Gold
- ☐ Grass
- ☐ Gravel
- ☐ Hoe
- ☐ Ice or snow
- ☐ Iron
- ☐ Ladder
- ☐ Leather
- ☐ Leaves
- ☐ Melon

- ☐ Pumpkin pie
- ☐ Saddle
- ☐ Sand
- ☐ Shovel
- ☐ Sign
- ☐ Spider eye
- ☐ Sponge
- ☐ Stairs
- ☐ Sticks
- ☐ Stone
- ☐ String
- ☐ Sugar
- ☐ Tree
- ☐ Vines

Mining and Crafting for Better Living

Every block, or material, that's mined in the game has a hardness level that determines which tool is best for breaking it. You can break most blocks by hand, without any tools, but using the right tool will save you lots of time. The general rules of thumb for using tools are shown on page 23.

Every player starts out with nothing in their inventory. The objective is to collect resources to craft a full set of tools so you can mine harder blocks to craft even stronger tools. Grab a tool and start breaking blocks!

1. When you first enter the game, you'll start at spawn point. Look around to see what types of resources are nearby. Start mining by punching trees to gather wood.

2. Turn the wood you've gathered into a crafting table, which allows you to craft all the tools available in the game (A). Without a crafting table, you're limited to crafting very few items. Start using your crafting table by turning your wood into tools, such as a pickaxe (B).

3. Build a shelter. Your shelter could be on top of a hill made from dirt or inside a mountain surrounded by stone blocks. If you're playing in survival mode, the goal is to build a shelter to protect you from monsters.

4. Craft a bed, if possible. You'll need three blocks of wool ("sheered" from sheep) of any color and three wood planks (C). Place the bed in a safe place, preferably inside a home (D). You can break the bed and take it with you when exploring further from home. If you don't make a bed, you can either hide out in your shelter or keep mining and fight any monsters that come your way.

5. Crafting a chest (E) is a great way to keep extra items (F). (In survival mode, players must craft all their resources; if they die, players lose all items in their inventory—unless they have placed them in the chest. In creative mode, players don't need chests, as you can't die and always have access to unlimited items.) Placing two chests next to each other creates one large chest.

✎ **GAME MODE**
Survival

⌛ **APPROXIMATE TIME TO COMPLETE**
1+ hours

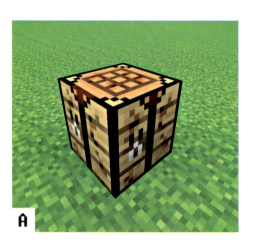
A

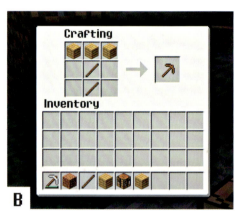
B

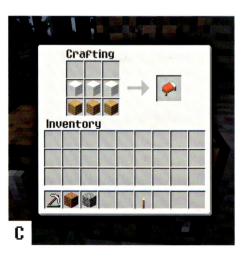
C

THE HARDER THE MATERIAL A TOOL IS MADE FROM, THE FASTER IT WILL BREAK BLOCKS.

HANDS (No Tools)	WOOD	STONE	IRON	GOLD	DIAMOND

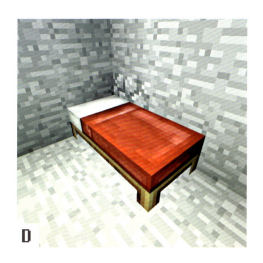

D

E

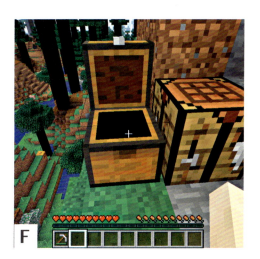

F

TOOLS CHEAT SHEET

Axes: for mining and crafting anything made from wood

Pickaxes: for mining and crafting stone or harder materials

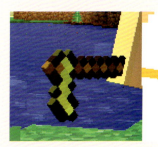

Shovels: for mining and crafting dirt

Hoes: for preparing the ground for planting

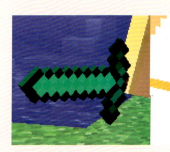

Weapons (such as swords): for killing mobs and animals

It's Electric!

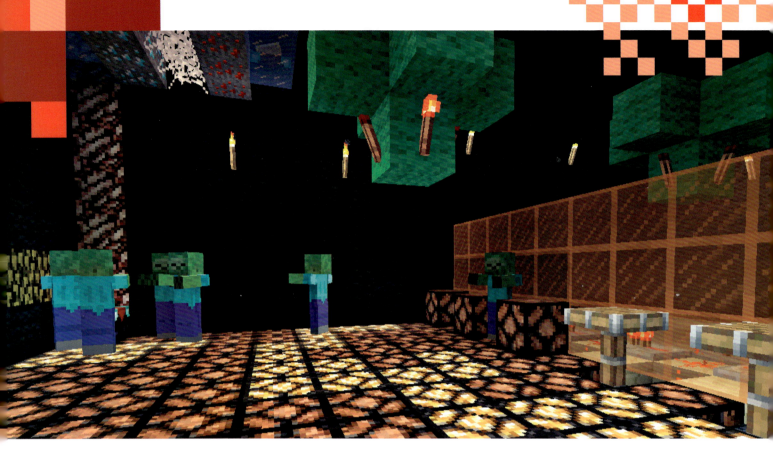

This lab is all about creating and conducting electricity. For the family activity, try your hand at creating a simple electrical circuit. For the Minecraft play, we explore redstone, which is used to create and conduct power. We use redstone dust to make a light-up dance floor and a disco ball, and to automate moving attractions. The goal is to create a party worthy of a mob—in this case, a mob of zombies. Zombies aren't always hostile—be sure to play in creative mode so they can't harm you!

FIND IT ONLINE

Check out this video to play with designing an electrical circuit: *bit.ly/3LpGnPb*.

MORE TO EXPLORE

+ How can you change or adapt your simple LED circuit into something different?

+ What happens when you use other types of batteries, like AA or AAA?

+ What happens when you add another switch to the circuit?

🧑‍🤝‍🧑 FAMILY ACTIVITY
Simple Circuit

Explore the basics of electricity with this fun project, in which you'll build a simple circuit using an LED light. You can purchase all the items you need at a hardware store.

⌛ APPROXIMATE TIME TO COMPLETE
1 hour

✂ MATERIALS
+ Wire cutter
+ 3-volt LED bulb
+ Button, coin, or watch cell battery
+ Electrical tape
+ Miniature toggle switch
+ Double-ended alligator clips (two clips connected by a wire)

1. Gather your materials (A). Use the wire cutter to expose the ends of both wires on the LED bulb. Trim the wires just enough so they're easy to work with, but without leaving too much wire exposed (B).

2. To make the bulb light up, connect the red (positive) wire to the positive side of the battery (the top cap), and the black (negative) wire to the negative side of the battery (the bottom cap). Use some electrical tape to make it stick (C).

3. Add a switch. To turn the bulb on and off, connect the bulb's black wire to one pole of the switch. Connect one of the black alligator clips to the other switch pole, and the other to the negative side of the battery (D).

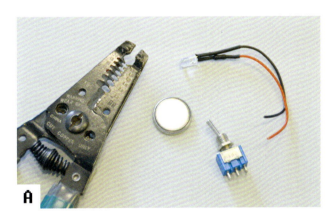
A

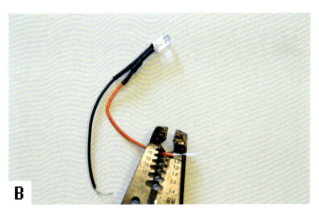
B

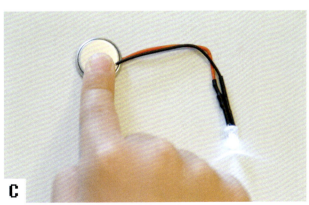
C

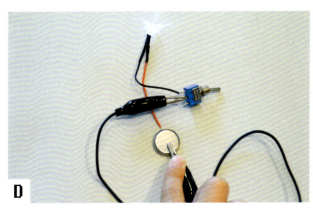
D

Zombie Dance Party

In this part of the lab, we create the decorations for a zombie party using redstone to build two different types of redstone clocks. These "clocks" are actually repeating circuits powered by redstone. One clock is used to power redstone lamps and sticky pistons (which can both push and pull blocks) to create a light-up dance floor, and the other is used to make a light-up entryway to the party.

1. Choose a flat world, then pick an area that will work for your dance club. To make the dance floor, dig out the floor at least two blocks down. Make a redstone clock using minecart rail, detector rail, powered rail, redstone torch, minecart, and redstone dust. Every revolution the cart makes sends a signal through the detector rail. The detector rail uses redstone dust to carry the signal to redstone lamps (on the left) and sticky pistons (on the right) (A).

✎ **GAME MODE**
Creative

⌛ **APPROXIMATE TIME TO COMPLETE**
2–3 hours; 15–30 minutes outside of Minecraft

ABOUT REDSTONE

Redstone is a main power source in Minecraft. It is like electricity and can transmit energy up to fifteen blocks away, though the energy weakens as it's transmitted over a distance.

FIND IT ONLINE

+ Check out Jesper the End's Minecraft disco party: *bit.ly/3Y2Q3GN.*
+ Here's a YouTube playlist to help inspire you: *bit.ly/4f7F70A.*

A

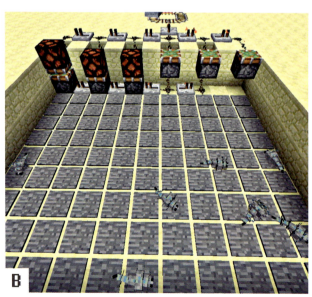

B

2. Place pressure plates all around the floor. Pressure plates have redstone functionality built into them. Once you have most of the floor covered, spawn several silverfish on top of the pressure plates and below the redstone lamps. The slippery bugs will light up the dance floor by activating the pressure plates as they roam around their dance floor cage (B). Place the redstone lamp above the plates, leaving enough room for the silverfish.

3. To make a disco ball, we added flickering redstone torches to prismarine brick blocks (C).

4. Finish your party by adding walls, other decorations, and music. We added a lighted entryway using redstone dust, redstone repeaters, and a redstone torch to create another type of redstone clock. Put redstone dust in your hand, break the torch, and quickly replace the torch with redstone dust (D). The zombies we invited can't wait for the party to start (E).

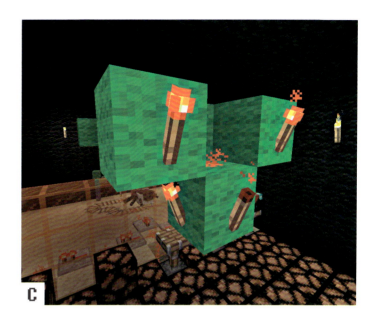

C

D

E

MORE TO EXPLORE

There are literally dozens of other ways to create a party in Minecraft. Have fun improvising!

+ We were inspired to create a zombie party, but you can invite any Minecraft character you like. Villagers look pretty funny with their arms crossed on the dance floor.

+ What other party features could you include? How about a smoke machine?

+ How can you add pyrotechnics to your party?

+ How would your party be different in survival mode?

+ What other mobs could you use to activate the pressure plates?

Setting a Trap

Kids love devising traps to snare the bad guys in Minecraft. Simple and efficient traps can be made quickly with just a few resources, while more advanced versions can take hours to design and build. To prepare for this challenge, the family activity will show players how to create a colorful Chinese finger trap.

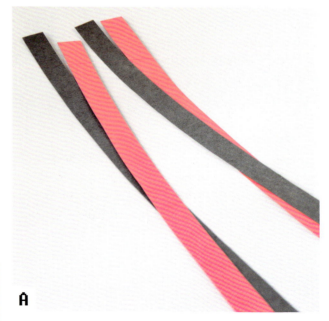

A

FIND IT ONLINE

For a tutorial on how to braid a finger trap, watch this YouTube video: *bit.ly/4f0apXa.*

🧍 FAMILY ACTIVITY
Chinese Finger Trap

The Chinese finger trap is a classic novelty toy that can confound those who try to escape its clutches. In this activity, each family member will make their own finger trap.

⌛ APPROXIMATE TIME TO COMPLETE

1 hour

✂ MATERIALS

+ Scissors
+ Construction paper in at least 2 colors
+ Transparent tape or glue
+ A thick marker or stick to braid the paper around

1. Cut four strips of paper, each approximately 12 inches (30.5 cm) long and 1 inch (2.5 cm) wide (A).

2. Tape or glue the ends of each pair of strips together at an angle of slightly less than 90 degrees (B).

3. To hold them temporarily in place, tape the corner of one pair of strips to the end of the marker or stick, then tape the second pair to the opposite side. Contrasting colors should appear next to each other, and the strips should be aligned (C).

4. Alternating colors, braid the strips around the marker or stick until you reach the end (D).

5. Use scissors to trim the braided ends, then tape or glue them together. Remove the tape from the end of the marker or stick. Pull the marker out of the center of the finger trap. Finish the ends with tape or glue (E).

🖥 MINECRAFT PLAY
Build a Zombie Trap

Lava is a block that's typically found deep underground, in pools of oozing magma, though sometimes it occurs above ground (in the Overworld) in lakes. Lava has many uses, but it's a well-known feature of monster traps. In this part of the lab, you'll build a beginner-level trap—a lava pit of doom—to lure, capture, and destroy hostile mobs and monsters.

1. Use a shovel to dig a pit three blocks by three blocks by three blocks. Place bedrock on the bottom of your pit to ensure that the lava will stay in place (A).

2. Locate a lava bucket in your inventory. Use the lava bucket to pour lava into the pit. Right-click to place the lava in the center of the bottom of the pit (B).

3. Hide the pit! Place dirt or grass blocks over the pit and put a trapdoor in the center. Position the trapdoor hinge opposite from the direction the monster will be approaching. Place a stone

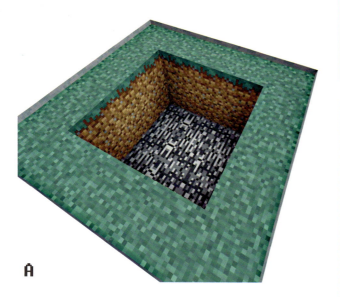

A

✎ GAME MODE
Build in creative or survival mode; play in survival mode.

⧖ APPROXIMATE TIME TO COMPLETE
1–2 hours

FIND IT ONLINE
The Minecraft Wiki is a great resource for trap ideas and for tutorials on building advanced traps: *bit.ly/4cAmMrx*.

MORE TO EXPLORE
Blocks of obsidian are created when flowing water comes into contact with lava. With obsidian, you can create a nether portal to use as part of your trap.

IT'S A TRAP!
These are some other Minecraft resources that are commonly used by trap makers:

+ Arrow dispensers
+ Pistons
+ Pressure plates
+ Sand
+ TNT
+ Trapdoors
+ Trip wire
+ Water

pressure plate in front of the trapdoor. In our build, the lava and the wall of the pit appear beneath the trapdoor (C).

4. Create a solid corridor that runs past the trap with a dead end just beyond it. Now it's time to place the bait—that's you! Get a monster to follow you down the corridor, and as you approach the pressure plate, leap to the other side. The monster will follow you, activate the trapdoor, and fall into the lava pit of doom (D). This basic trap works for both creepers and zombies.

5. Follow the link opposite, left, to discover more advanced ways to trap monsters and capture their loot at the same time.

SHARE YOUR WORK
Sharing imaginative trap designs is very popular online. There are hundreds of examples on YouTube and on blogs. Record the steps you took to create your trap and share them, along with screenshots, on your family blog.

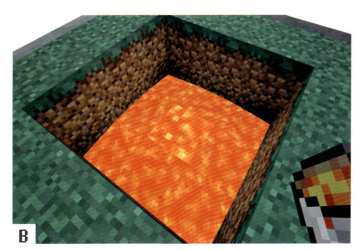

B

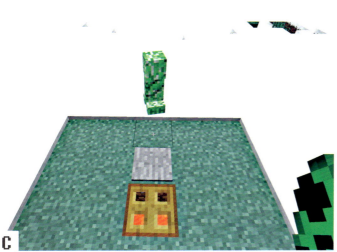

C

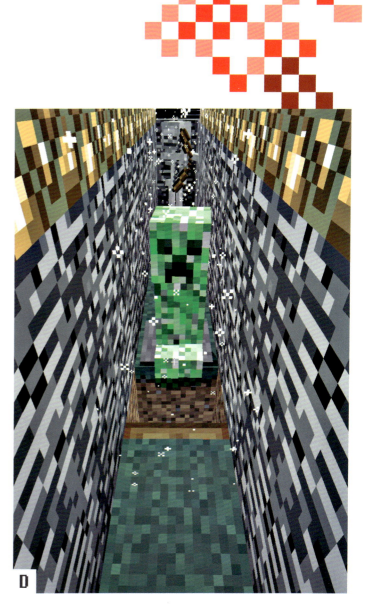

D

Fire When Ready!

In this lab you'll alternate between dodging marshmallows and firing TNT into a medieval fortress. In the family activity, you'll have some fun building a Popsicle stick catapult, while in Minecraft, you'll get acquainted with one of the more popular blocks in your inventory—TNT! TNT is a special block that, when ignited with flint and steel, will explode and destroy blocks located near it (the image above shows an explosion in process). For more details, see the sidebar "Getting to Know TNT in Minecraft," page 35.

Marshmallow Catapult

⏳ **APPROXIMATE TIME TO COMPLETE**
30 minutes

✂ **MATERIALS**
+ 7 large Popsicle sticks, 6 inches (15 cm) long
+ 10 to 12 rubber bands
+ Plastic spoon
+ Marshmallows

1. Stack five sticks on top of each other and secure both ends of the stack with rubber bands (A).

2. Secure the plastic spoon to one of the remaining sticks with at least three rubber bands (B).

3. Attach the remaining stick beneath the stick with the spoon at the bottom only using a rubber band (C). Make sure to leave one end open.

4. Finally, pry open and then slide the end of the launcher around the stack of sticks and securely attach the two components with rubber bands across the center (D). Cross at least two rubber bands to secure the catapult to the base.

5. Load a marshmallow onto your catapult and fire away!

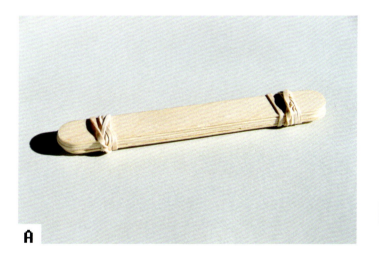

A

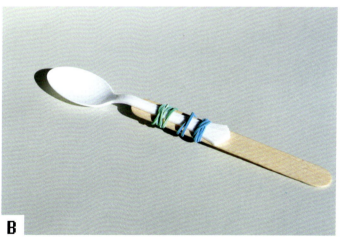

B

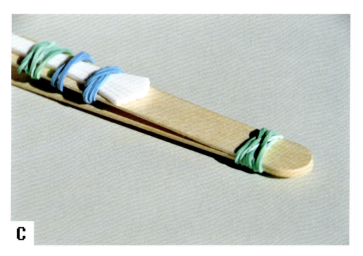

C

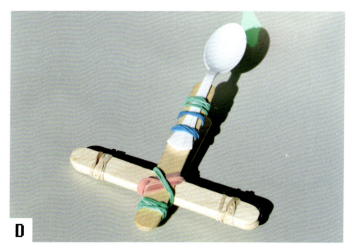

D

Building and Firing a Cannon with TNT

In this part of the lab, you'll build a basic cannon that fires a block of TNT into the distance. The TNT will explode in the air or on the ground. After you've built your first cannon, experiment by adjusting the amount of TNT you use, or build your cannon on the edge of a mountaintop to increase its firing range. See page 35, for more on how TNT works in Minecraft.

1. Using stone blocks, build two short walls, each one block high and nine blocks long. Build the walls parallel to each other and one block apart. Close off the narrow area between them at one end with another block of stone. The TNT will be launched from the open end (A).

2. At the closed end of the foundation, place two blocks of stone, one on top of the other. Destroy the block on the bottom (the one touching the ground) and fill the cavity with water. The water should flow all the way to the end of the wall but not beyond it (B). Adding water to the bottom of the cannon will ensure that it won't explode when the TNT is ignited.

3. Place the lever or button behind the tall block at the closed end of the cannon. Connect the lever to redstone wire. Run the wire along most of the length of both walls. Stop the wire one block short of the end of the wall on the right and two blocks short of the end of the wall on the left (C).

✎ **GAME MODE**
Creative

⌛ **APPROXIMATE TIME TO COMPLETE**
2 hours

🖥 **INVENTORY REQUIREMENTS**
+ Stone blocks
+ Bucket of water
+ Lever or button
+ Redstone wire
+ Stone slab
+ Four redstone repeaters
+ TNT

FIND IT ONLINE
Do you want to discover five more ways to make a cannon? Check out this video: *bit.ly/3W4qYbI*.

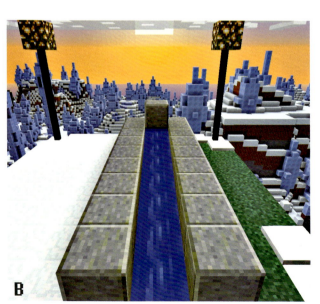

B

4. At the open end of the cannon, place the slab on top of the water block and add two more stone blocks to the wall to the left of the slab. Add redstone wire on top of those blocks (D). These blocks will prime the TNT just before it's launched into the air. When primed, or activated with redstone, TNT blocks blink white.

5. Place four repeaters along the left wall and set the delay on each to at least two ticks (E). Repeaters slow down the signal from the lever just a bit so the TNT block is launched before it explodes.

6. Make sure the redstone lever is disengaged, then fill the water cavity with TNT blocks (F). Pull the switch! The blocks of TNT will explode, launching the solitary TNT block at the open end of the cannon into the air.

GETTING TO KNOW TNT IN MINECRAFT

Most commonly activated with flint and steel

+ Won't destroy blocks under water

+ Useful for clearing out large areas

+ Use redstone to wire cannons, traps, and other crafty innovations

+ Can be placed in a minecart and sent down the rail line as an explosive surprise

+ Can be placed next to each other to create colossal explosions

MORE TO EXPLORE

Have each family or team member build a fortress around their cannon and see whose can survive the longest.

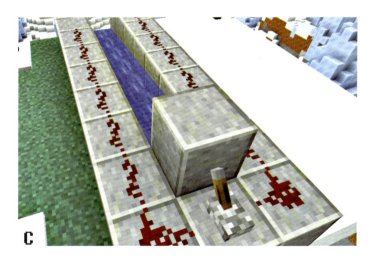

C

D

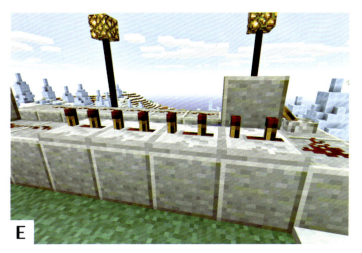

E

F

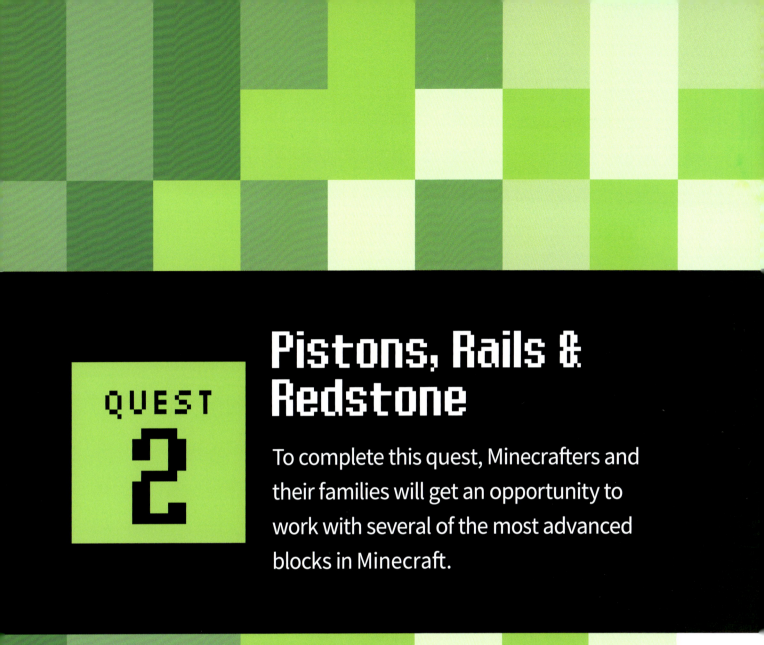

Pistons, Rails & Redstone

To complete this quest, Minecrafters and their families will get an opportunity to work with several of the most advanced blocks in Minecraft.

Redstone Laboratory

re you a fan of fun science shows that test out crazy ideas? In this in-game activity, you'll set up your own redstone-powered science laboratory where you'll run experiments and use as a hub for future labs. The lab will feature redstone mechanisms and solar sensors to automate doors, turn lights on and off, play notes when someone visits, and notify you when it's safe to go outside.

In the hands-on activity, you'll construct a solar telescope that can be used to safely make observations of the surface of the Sun.

WHAT'S THE SCIENCE?

By allowing a tight beam of light to enter the box, which produces a remarkably sharp and accurate image of the Sun, a solar telescope allows us to look at the Sun safely. **It's NEVER safe to look directly at the Sun** because its light and energy are intensified by the cells of our retinas, at the backs of our eyes. Those cells are very sensitive to light and help us see things when light levels are low. Looking directly at the Sun can burn and even destroy this very important part of our eyes.

👥 FAMILY ACTIVITY

Solar Telescope

The Sun provides us not only with light, but with energy as well. In this activity, you'll build a solar telescope that will safely allow you to look at the Sun's reflection.

⌛ APPROXIMATE TIME TO COMPLETE
30 minutes

✂ MATERIALS
+ Multipurpose tape
+ Cardboard box with lid
+ White paper
+ Scissors
+ Pen
+ Sewing needle

1. Using the multipurpose tape, cover all sources of light inside the box and lid. Tape the sheet of white paper to the inside of the box at one end (A).

2. Place the lid on the box. Identify a location about one-third of the way down from the end opposite the paper. Draw an egg-shaped outline that approximates the width of your face. Next, cut around the outline you drew (B). You'll place your forehead through this hole, so make sure it's wide enough to see through. To ensure that as little light as possible enters the box, apply tape around the edges of the hole.

3. Place the lid tightly on the box. In the box end opposite the paper, push the needle through the box and/or the tape and pull it out the other side (C). The cleaner the hole you create, the sharper the image will be.

4. Your solar telescope is complete. With the lid firmly in place, point the pinhole in the direction of the Sun and place your eyes through the opening in the lid (D).

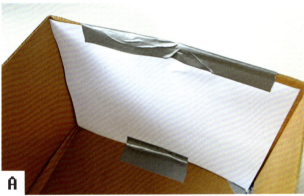

A

B

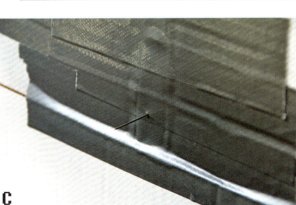

C

D

Science Laboratory

Start your Minecraft STEM journey by building a crazy science laboratory and installing at least three mechanisms:

- **Daylight sensors** to turn the lights on when it gets dark and to play a sound to notify you when the Sun is coming up.

- **A doorbell** that will play a lovely tune when your guests arrive.

- **Piston tables** to set your lab equipment on.

1. Create a new Minecraft world in creative mode to use for exploring the labs in this book. Find a location with access to an ocean or a river and that has some flat space and several biomes nearby. Locate a spot for your laboratory. Sketch a blueprint for your building in a notebook.

2. Level out an area to build upon and construct your lab, keeping these guidelines in mind:
- Scientists need clean, open space to work in.
- Scientists spend a lot of time making observations, so include windows.
- You'll need a flat roof with access (stairs) from below. Make sure your roof is at least two blocks thick (A).

3. First, let's set up a daylight sensor and two note blocks in a series. At first light, the sensor will signal the note blocks to play two notes to notify the hardworking scientists that it's daytime. On your roof, set up your materials in the following order: daylight sensor, redstone dust, note block sitting on top of a gold block, a repeater, and then another note block sitting on top of a gold block (B).

4. Right-click on each note block and you will hear a pleasant chime. Additional right-clicks will adjust the pitch of each note. Place the repeater in line with the note blocks. Adjust the signal delay by right-clicking the redstone torch on the repeater one, two, or three times. You can add more repeaters to delay the note even longer. In image B, the circuit is active and the repeater is set to maximum delay. Tip: You can use a switch in place of the sensor to test your system. When it sounds perfect, replace the switch with the sensor and wait for the Sun to rise.

✎ GAME MODE
Creative

⧗ APPROXIMATE TIME TO COMPLETE
2+ hours

FIND IT ONLINE

Want to add even more cool features to your lab? Check out 30+ Science Laboratory builds here: https://bit.ly/3XyZKw8.

A

5. Next, you'll attach a sensor to a "not gate," which will produce a signal when the sensor is not active at nightfall. In other words, the not gate will turn the lights on at dusk and will keep them on until the Sun rises.

6. As an experiment, set up a simple not gate between a sensor and a redstone lamp in the following order: daylight sensor, redstone dust, an opaque block like quartz with a redstone torch attached on the opposite side away from the sensor, more redstone dust, and then the redstone lamp. Test two different "not gate" setups to see how they work (C, D).

(continued)

B

C

D

7. You can now recreate this sequence on your roof. Our example (E, F) shows what your automatic lighting should look like from the top of the roof and from underneath it. We've connected ten redstone lamps to one daylight sensor and one not gate. Determine where you want to place your lamps and personalize your automated lighting system.

8. To make a musical note doorbell, you'll need a switch, note blocks, red stone dust, and repeaters. Place the note blocks on top of blocks of your choice to recreate different instruments. Visit *bit.ly/3zCBQ9k* to see a selection of instruments you can choose from. Redstone dust may be placed only on a flat surface, or it can run down a block like a staircase. Note blocks will work only if there is a block of air above them, so you will need to dig a pit at least three blocks deep in front of and below your doorbell (G). When placing repeaters, the stationary redstone torch should be placed opposite the switch in the direction the signal is traveling (H). (In the top setup, the note block will not work because the redstone torch on the repeater faces toward the lever. In the bottom setup, the torch correctly faces toward the note block.) You can cover up the surface of the pit when finished, but make sure each note block has an air block above it and there are no blocks directly on top of your redstone wiring.

E

F

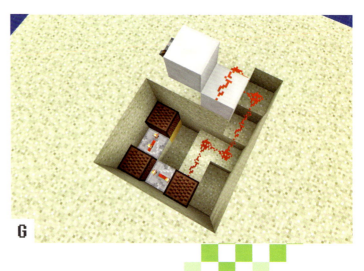

G

9. You'll need lots of workspace inside your laboratory. Place several pistons around your lab and activate each by placing a redstone torch beneath them (I). You can use regular or sticky pistons for tables. Tip: Place slabs around the pistons to create a slightly elevated floor. Your new tables will now be at the perfect height.

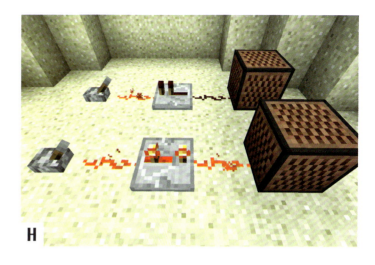

H

10. Your laboratory is mostly complete, so now it is time to add some finishing touches. What kinds of equipment do scientists need in a laboratory? We've included brewing stands, a furnace, lab tables, a fish tank, and windows the color of a rainbow. We decorated our lab with item frames containing blocks like ores, plants, items found in rivers and oceans, and a bunch of redstone (J). What did we miss?

I

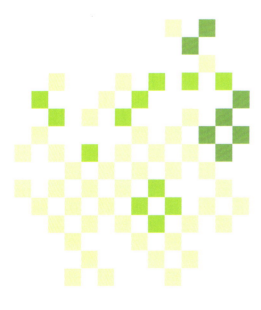

J

All Aboard

Welcome aboard! In this lab, you'll build a railroad to transport visitors and supplies throughout your realm. You'll learn how to automate much of your system, and create a mini Grand Central Station near your laboratory. Out-of-game, you'll build a giant marble roller coaster that tests the boundaries of physics!

FIND IT ONLINE

You'll love this creative coaster made from paper rolls: *bit.ly/4cXuxHB*.

WHAT'S THE SCIENCE?

It's all about energy. Everything has stored energy called potential energy. The marble is waiting for a push to release its energy. The energy it releases is called kinetic energy, sometimes referred to as movement energy, which can be transformed into other kinds of energy used by humans to power up.

FAMILY ACTIVITY

Make a Roller Coaster

This requires a real team effort and keen design and engineering skills, so gather as many family and friends as you can.

⌛ APPROXIMATE TIME TO COMPLETE
1–2 hours

✂ MATERIALS
+ ¾-inch (2 cm)-wide flexible foam tubing, enough to complete your design
+ Scissors
+ Multipurpose or masking tape
+ Assorted props such as books, pots, cardboard tubes, and plastic cups to elevate your rail
+ Marbles
+ Graph paper to sketch your design (optional)

1. Flexible foam tubing usually comes preslit down the length of one side. Run the scissors carefully along the seam to open it completely, then turn it 180 degrees and cut the split tubing lengthwise until it separates into two equal pieces. Connect each section of tubing at the underside only (A). Adding tape to the top of the rail may impede the marble.

2. Your coaster should begin at a high point but, ultimately, make its way to the ground. Along the way it can speed up, slow down, and even change direction. Experiment by adding supports and fun features like bridges, curves, and tunnels (B).

3. You can take better advantage of limited space by designing several changes of direction in your coaster. Test out designs to see which one best switches the marble from one track to another (C).

4. After final assembly, give it a go! Our patio table was the perfect spot (D). If running along a wall, be sure to use wall-safe tape. You'll likely need plenty of tape.

A

B

C

D

Rail System

Your challenge is to make a rail system that begins at your science lab and takes you, or your cargo, on a tour of each biome. You may want to take riders in a loop, beginning and ending at your lab, or allow them to hop on and off at two or more stations.

1. Construct a one-way station everywhere you think visitors may want to explore (A). Create this single-stop station by digging a hole one block deep and two blocks wide. Place two powered rails inside the hole and connect one end with normal rails. Place any block of your choice on ground level, adjacent to the pit. Place a button on the block facing the powered rails (A). Finally, place a minecart on one of the powered rails, push the button, and off you go! Connect each station to your system.

2. A two-way station is handy when you want to allow riders the option of choosing a direction to travel. Follow the directions in step 1 to create a one-way station, but you'll also need to place a lever within reach at the intersection of the rail line (B). Before pushing the button to go, riders will pull the lever to set the direction of travel.

3. Detector rails activate mechanisms like note blocks, redstone lamps, and command blocks. Place one detector rail in your line and run redstone dust from it to a mechanism of your choice. When the cart rolls on top of it, the mechanism is activated (C) to alert you that a minecart is coming.

4. Use a detector rail and a command block to teleport you to your front door when your journey ends. Set it up like the example in step 3, but replace the note block with a command block. Get a command block by typing
- /give @p minecraft:command_block
- Walk over to the front door of your lab and press F3. Look for XYZ followed by three numbers, which identify your location. Write them down.

✎ **GAME MODE**
Creative

⧗ **APPROXIMATE TIME TO COMPLETE**
2 hours

INVENTORY REQUIREMENTS
+ Normal rails
+ Powered rails (increases minecart speed if powered with redstone)
+ One or more note blocks
+ Buttons, levers, and trip wire
+ Minecarts
+ Detector rails (activates a redstone mechanism when a minecart passes over it)
+ Redstone dust and redstone torches
+ A command block (issues commands to the server)
+ One dispenser filled with minecarts

A

B

C

5. Place and connect your command block with redstone dust to the detector rail. Right-click on the command block and in the box type in the following, replacing XYZ with your coordinates. Leave a space between each coordinate:

- /tp @p x y z
- Click DONE.

6. Test it out by hopping into a minecart and riding over the detector rail. You should be transported to your front door. We didn't want a bunch of empty minecarts lying around, so we added a lava pit at the end of the line (D).

7. Call a minecart to your front door by connecting a pressure plate to a dispenser filled with minecarts. Connect the dispenser to your rail line with powered rails and normal rails. The powered rails need a redstone lamp next to them or below them to activate. We added a waypoint so that the cart stops in front of the lab, allowing you to hop aboard (E).

8. Use a trip wire to automatically switch rail direction. Carts with cargo will go one way and riders will go another. Connect the trip wire between two blocks that are at least three blocks apart. Both trip wire mechanisms need to be two blocks high with the rail between them (F). With wire in your hand, right-click on the mechanism to attach.

9. Working on the other side of the mechanism, connect the right trip wire to the rail that is at the junction of your two lines. In our example, riders will travel left and cargo will continue ahead (G). Test your system. As players activate the trip wire, the redstone will engage and switch them to the left track. Minecarts with cargo will slip under the trip wire and continue straight ahead.

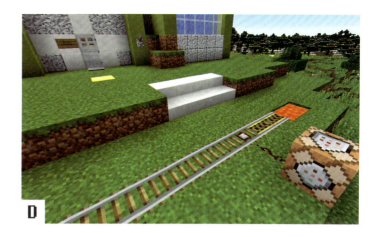

D

E

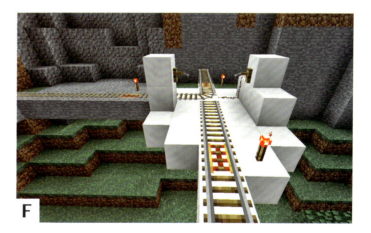

F

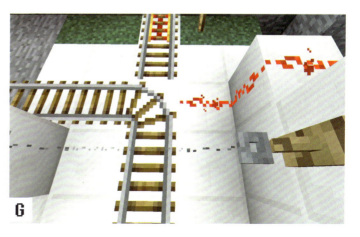

G

NOW TRY THIS

For players seeking more of a challenge:
+ After learning more about pistons and trapdoors in Lab 8, add a secret entrance to your lab.
+ Create more elaborate tunes for your note block doorbell.
+ Build an observatory building on top of your roof.

Gravity Impact

In this lab, you'll test gravity in and out of game. In-game, you'll measure and test the effect gravity has on objects; in the family activity, you'll measure Earth's gravity by observing the impact of items landing in a soft substance.

FIND IT ONLINE
Watch Nanogirl demonstrate how to overcome the force of gravity: *bit.ly/4cUw4yb*.

🧑 FAMILY ACTIVITY
Testing the Effects of Gravity

Record the impact of several items dropped onto a bed of flour.

⏳ APPROXIMATE TIME TO COMPLETE
30 minutes

✂ MATERIALS
+ Scoop
+ Flour
+ Tray
+ Ruler
+ Data table for recording your results
+ 4 or 5 objects of different sizes and weights, like rocks, marbles, and a bouncy ball

1. Scoop about 3 cups (360 g) of flour onto your tray. (Note: The flour will dust the surrounding surface as you conduct your experiment!) Use the scoop to smooth out the flour base. Measure and record the depth of the flour base (A).

2. Drop one item at a time. Use a ruler to measure the depth and diameter of the crater from each impact, then smooth out the flour to prepare for the next object (B).

3. Log your findings in a notebook. Use a table like the one shown below, to keep track of them. Jot down other observations to record as much as possible during the experiment.

A

B

OBJECT	SIZE OF OBJECT	CRATER DEPTH	CRATER DIAMETER	OTHER OBSERVATIONS
Large bouncy ball	6 inches (15 cm)	1 inch (2.5 cm)	4 inches (10 cm)	The large, yellow bouncy ball hit the flour surface and then bounced off and onto the floor.
Rock	2 inches (5 cm)	1¼ inches (3.2 cm)	2¾ inches (7 cm)	The rock made a larger cloud of flour than the bouncy ball.
Building-block toy	1 inch (2.5 cm)	1 inch (2.5 cm)	1½ inches (4 cm)	The flour got stuck inside the holes of the building block toy.

Gravity in Minecraft

Every Minecrafter knows there's something strange about in-game gravity. Falling block items like sand, gravel, and concrete powder are subject to its force, but when stones and trees are mined, they mysteriously defy it. In this activity, you'll test the effect of gravity in Minecraft. Experiment by activating a redstone lamp with different inputs, including dropped items, tower height, redstone signal length, and type of redstone block. Keep track of your data, just as you did in the family activity.

GAME MODE
Creative

APPROXIMATE TIME TO COMPLETE
45 minutes

1. Build a tower of blocks to measure distance more easily. Colored wool works great for the tower. We alternated between yellow and black wool (A).

2. Place a wooden pressure plate at the base of the tower. Connect the pressure plate with one piece of redstone dust to any redstone-activated block, like a piston or lamp (B).

3. To help make the drops consistent, build an automatic dropping mechanism. Start by building a 2 × 10 block vertical wall two blocks to the left of your colored block tower. The wall will allow you to add slabs that will hold the redstone dust (C).

4. Place the stone slabs on the 2 × 10 wall in an offset pattern. Make sure the lowest slab is an inverted slab; it shouldn't be touching the ground. Place your first slab on the top half of your lower-left block wall (D). Our redstone ladder uses quartz slabs.

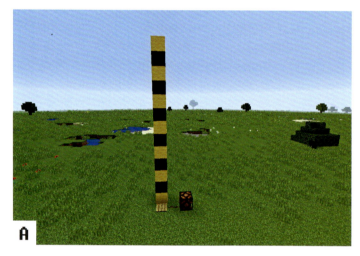

A

B

5. Add redstone dust on top of each slab. Place a piston facing toward the measurement tower on the top slab. At the base of the ladder, place redstone on the ground and a redstone repeater to boost the redstone signal (E). There are different types of redstone ladders; try your hand at designing a different version.

6. Flip your lever to activate the piston. The piston pushes a block to fall along the wall. Compare gravel, sand, concrete powder, and the anvil using your simple remote-drop mechanism. Change the distance from your pressure plate to the redstone lamp. Adjust the height of your simple drop mechanism. Switch your pressure plate with different types of pressure plates. Do the blocks fall at different speeds? What happens to the blocks when they drop (F)?

NOW TRY THIS

+ Does gravity affect objects differently if they're tied together? What if they were loosely tied together? Craft a wireless redstone contraption using a command block and the /setblock command.

+ Build a vacuum chamber to demonstrate the force of gravity without air resistance.

+ Try the Anti-Gravity Star-Miner mod available for the Java edition of Minecraft.

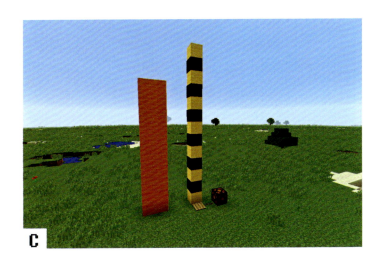

C

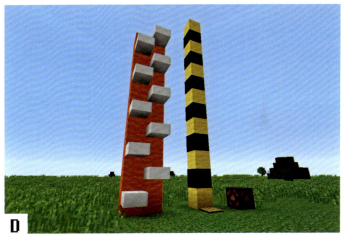

D

E

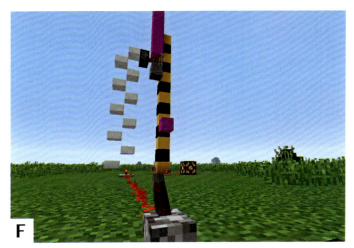

F

Piston Power

Most commonly found inside an internal combustion engine, pistons move up and down and turn a shaft that eventually propels a vehicle. The key benefit of a hydraulic piston is the mechanical advantage—the amount of force—gained by using it, since pressure within the system can't be lost. (See "What's the Science?" for more information.)

In the hands-on activity, build a piston using simple household materials. In-game, explore piston traps to protect your home from pesky mobs.

WHAT'S THE SCIENCE?

Scientist Blaise Pascal (1623–1662) discovered the law of fluid pressure, also known as Pascal's principle, when the pressure applied to one side of a closed system containing fluid and pistons is transferred to the other side of the system undiminished because the pressure within the system is equal. We can change the mechanical advantage by changing the size of the system and the distance the fluid travels.

Hydraulic Pistons

Create a hydraulic piston with a balloon, baggie, and hose, then test it to see how much it can lift. Does it require more, less, or the same amount of force to lift the objects?

⧗ APPROXIMATE TIME TO COMPLETE
30 minutes

✂ MATERIALS
+ Small tubing or hose (we used aquarium airline tubing)
+ 1 plastic zippered snack baggie
+ Water
+ 1 balloon
+ Packing tape
+ 2 empty plastic containers
+ A selection of small objects

A

1. Gather up your supplies to make your own hydraulic piston. If you don't have a balloon, you can substitute a zippered baggie (A). If you're using a balloon, blow into it to soften it up, to allow for easier movement of the water.

2. Slip one end of the tubing through the zippered opening in the baggie. Slip the other end into the balloon. Make sure the tubing extends far down into both the balloon and the baggie (B).

B

3. Seal the balloon with tape first, then fill the baggie with water, zip it closed, and seal it well with tape. Place the balloon and baggie in separate plastic containers, which can act as supports for larger items like books and rocks, then test the seal on the baggie by pressing down on it (C). Water will pour out of a poorly sealed baggie. If needed, refill the baggie with water and fix the seal before continuing to the next step.

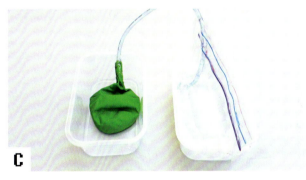

C

4. Start with a light object on top of the balloon. Slowly press down on the plastic baggie full of water and watch as the balloon fills with water and lifts the item (D). Start with something light, then try heavier objects like books or rocks to see how much your hydraulic piston can lift.

D

Redstone Pistons

The piston appears to be a simple block that just pushes and pulls things, but it really can be used for much more. Hydraulic pistons don't exist in Minecraft; rather, pistons use the mysterious electrical power from redstone. In this activity, we build a few variations of redstone piston contraptions, including a Jeb trap.

1. Build a 4 × 9-wide pit three blocks deep. One block in from the sides, place eight horizontal sticky pistons that will retract to pull the middle parts back. Check the image for the clever blocks around the bottom that will hold redstone and the sticky pistons (A).

2. Place four sticky pistons pointing vertically next to the lower horizontal pistons. These pistons will hold blocks that look like the ground. Place redstone repeaters behind the upper horizontal sticky pistons. Drop redstone dust around the edges to connect all the pistons (B). This is the most complicated part of the Jeb-trap build. Take your time. The trap will work; just follow what you see in the images. If it doesn't work, check your redstone connections. You may need to add a repeater to carry the redstone signal further.

3. The Jeb trap is now complete and ready to be activated. We used prismarine blocks to make the floor more obvious during the build. Switch out the prismarine for grass blocks for a truly incognito trap (C). Jeb traps have been around a long time. Although they look complicated, with a few practice attempts, you'll be a pro.

✏ GAME MODE
Creative

⌛ APPROXIMATE TIME TO COMPLETE
1 hour

A

FIND IT ONLINE
Check out Mumbo Jumbo's video on ten simple piston doors: *bit.ly/3LlUOUo.*

4. With the Jeb trap deactivated, dig down several block layers to add lava or water at the bottom to capture creepers, zombies, and other hostile mobs.

5. Find a regular-looking hill or mountain for the super-secret simple fortress. Dig out an interior and design the inside of your new cave.

6. Place two horizontal sticky pistons in the entrance to your mountain cave. Use the same block found in the mountain to stick on the end of the sticky piston. When the piston is deactivated, the piston retracts and reveals a simple two-block door (D). This method of hiding your door may be a temporary fix while you craft a more permanent solution on your server.

7. Place a lever on the block next to the sticky pistons. Use your stealth skills to hide the lever. Place a temporary block in front of the lever to effectively hide it (E). Jot down the coordinates to make sure you remember the location of the secret door.

NOW TRY THIS

+ How much can your hydraulic piston lift? What can you do to make it lift ten times as much?

+ How might you apply your knowledge of pistons from this lab for use in the Chain Reaction Contraption (see Lab 22)?

+ Where else could you use a Jeb trap? How would it work if it were mounted vertically?

B

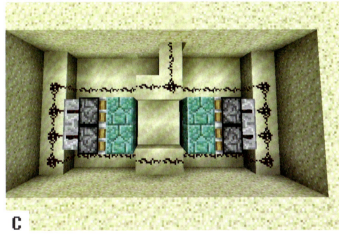

C

D

E

QUEST

3

Creative Thinking

In this quest, create gardens, design flying machines that defy the forces of gravity, build a figure of your favorite Minecraft character, and become a puppeteer.

Grow a Garden

Plants in Minecraft act similarly to plants out of the game. Both require sufficient sunlight, water, and prepared soil. Both start from seeds and, when harvested, give seeds in return. Plants outside the game use photosynthesis to produce their own food from sunlight. Plants in the game also require sunlight to grow. The farther your plants are from water, the slower they grow. As an example, wheat takes about forty minutes of gameplay to grow from seed to harvestable crop. Of course, there are ways to make your crops grow faster, in and out of the game.

In this lab, you'll grow plants in and out of the game as a way to connect gameplay with real life.

🨚 FAMILY ACTIVITY
Planting Seeds

Help your Minecraft-loving counterpart learn about growing plants in this family activity. Pick out seeds appropriate for the growing season, plant them, and observe them as they grow. Try experimenting with different seeds, soil, and water content. Take some time to garden. Whether you're planning a new garden or maintaining an existing one, this lab offers the chance to spend time outdoors.

⧗ APPROXIMATE TIME TO COMPLETE
30 minutes

✂ MATERIALS
+ Pot
+ Soil
+ Packet of seeds
+ Water

1. Prepare the soil. Fill a garden pot with soil most of the way to the top. The soil should be rich in color and ready for your seeds and water.

2. Use a finger or a tool to poke a hole into the soil. Drop a couple of seeds into the hole and cover with soil. Water the seeds and place in sufficient sunlight (A). Get your hands dirty by planting seeds in a garden pot, then give your plants the water and sun they need to grow.

A

Sow, Grow, Harvest

Time to build a garden in Minecraft. Craft a hoe out of any material you have available. Use the hoe to prepare the ground for your garden. Once you've used the hoe, pour water within a couple of blocks of your crop. For efficient use of crop watering, place the crops in rows with water in between.

✏ GAME MODE
Creative

⧗ APPROXIMATE TIME TO COMPLETE
1 hour

1. Potatoes, wheat, carrots, melons, and pumpkins are food staples inside the game. Potatoes can be found at automatically generated NPC (nonplayer character) villages and, more rarely, by killing a zombie. An easy way to collect wheat seeds is to break tall grass.

2. Craft a hoe using sticks and wood, iron, stone, gold, or diamonds (A). The material you pick will be subject to wearing down as it is used. Hoes are only for preparing the ground for planting, so you won't need to craft many for a typical size garden. Right-click on the ground to prepare the soil for seeds.

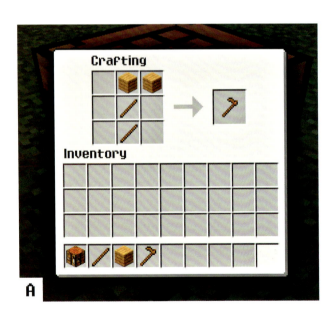

A

B

3. Bone meal is your secret growth-hacking tool. Bone meal can be crafted from bones (B). One bone gives you three bone meals. With bone meal, most plants will grow almost instantly. Gather bones by killing skeletons. Without bone meal, your crops will take a few day/night cycles to grow to the harvestable stage (C). In our example, the left row has been fertilized with bone meal. The other two rows have been left to grow naturally.

4. Once the crop is fully grown, left-click on the plant to harvest. Beware: wandering mobs can destroy your garden. Protect your crops with walls of iron bars (D) or any other block that will keep mobs out.

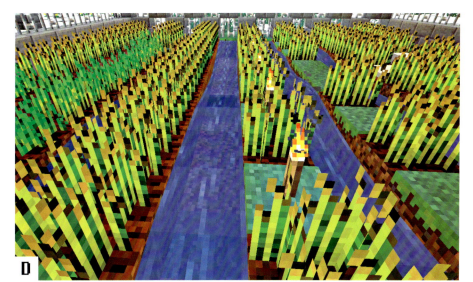

MORE TO EXPLORE

+ Bone meal can also be used to create dye. Place bone meal in the center of the crafting table and a chunk of lapis lazuli to craft blue dye. Bone meal is an essential ingredient for crafting a white firework star.

+ Try your hand at automatic farming. You can use a piston system that drops water on the crops to automatically harvest all the plants.

+ The garden shown above was designed to promote rapid growth and easy access for harvesting. Because snow can hurt crops and freeze water, torches were placed nearby to keep them warm.

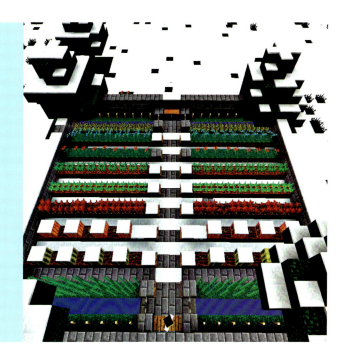

Flying Machine

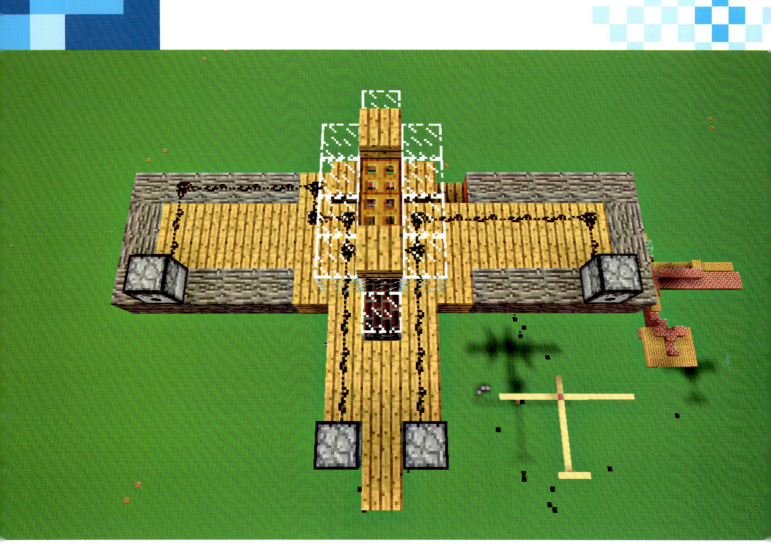

Paper airplanes have a long history that goes back to the manufacture of paper and the art of origami in China and perhaps Japan. Leonardo da Vinci wrote of a parchment aircraft and tested paper versions of his ornithopter, an aircraft that flew by flapping its wings like a bird.

In this lab, you'll fold and fly paper airplanes in the family activity, then let your imagination run wild while crafting airships inside of Minecraft.

Paper Airplanes

You may be familiar with paper airplanes, such as the classic dart, condor, delta wing, bullet, and stealth bomber, or even experimentals like the flying ring. In this family activity you'll have the chance to craft a few paper airplanes for a fun family flying competition. Ready to put your imaginative flying designs to the test?

⏳ **APPROXIMATE TIME TO COMPLETE**
30 minutes

✂ **MATERIALS**
+ Several sheets of paper, 8-1/2 x 11 inches (21.6 x 27.9 cm)

1. Build several paper airplane models (A).

2. Set the flying arena. It could be a hallway, sidewalk, or backyard. Set a line to throw behind and check that the wind is calm.

3. Try out these paper airplane challenges: longest distance, shortest distance, longest timed flight, shortest timed flight, wackiest flight, highest flight, and the near-miss flight. The winner of the near-miss flight challenge will have a plane that almost crashes yet continues its flight.

4. Once you've tried making and flying a classic paper airplane, try customizing by adding flaps, rudders, elevators, and weights to improve the design.

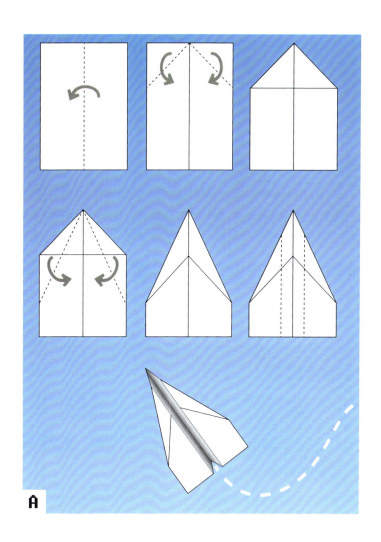

A

FIND IT ONLINE

There are hundreds of different types of paper airplanes that are ready to be put to the challenge. Check out this site for templates: *bit.ly/3VYUoYV.*

MORE TO EXPLORE

Takuo Toda holds the world record of 27.9 seconds for the longest time his paper airplane was in the air. Dillon Ruble holds the distance record of over 289 feet (88 m).

It's a Bird, It's a Plane, It's Minecraft Airships!

There are many different types of airships that have been crafted inside of Minecraft. Blimps, spaceships, airplanes, kites, helicopters, birds, magic carpets, and superheroes are just a few of the flying creations people have made inside of Minecraft.

1. Build a column of blocks. Use any type of block to build to a height of your choice.

2. From the top of the column start building your airship. Build the bottom of the fuselage, then move on to the wings (A). Our glider is almost ready for liftoff.

3. Break the column. Minecraft offers us a little bit of magic at this step. Once you've built the column, you can break the lower blocks while the rest float in the air. Your airship will have the appearance of floating (B).

✎ **GAME MODE**
Creative

⌛ **APPROXIMATE TIME TO COMPLETE**
2–3 hours

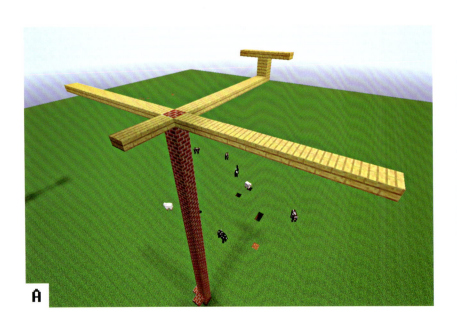

A

MORE TO EXPLORE

Another way to play: You and your team can keep the list handy during the week and take pictures of the items whenever and wherever you find them. Post the craziest pictures (especially the spider eye) to your blog.

4. Build more airships. A single airship is nice, but it's even cooler to have a fleet of ships. Imagine a favorite book, TV show, or movie as you create a fleet of custom airships. You're limited only by your imagination. Try a squadron of funky airships (C), or a ship built with redstone-activated dispensers (D).

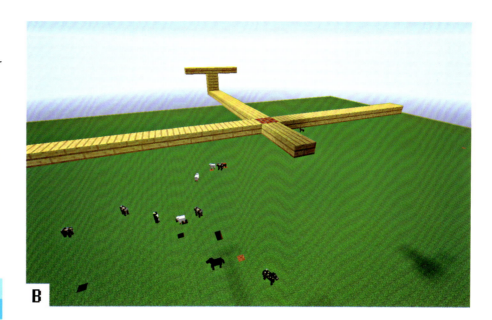

B

SHARE YOUR WORK

+ The easiest way to share your airship is by taking a screenshot and posting it online. Use a screen recording program to create a video tour and share it on YouTube.

+ Using the mod MCedit, you can copy and paste schematics into your world. Schematics are builds that people have created and share online by allowing others to download and paste into their own games. Do a web search for "schematics airships Minecraft" and you'll find lots of great options.

+ If you're ready for the next step, you can make and share a schematic of your airship.

C

D

Creating Figures

In the game, you and your family will work together to design a museum or cultural center that you can use for the entire quest. Throughout the space, you'll need enough room for statues on pedestals, paintings in frames, a stage for performance, and a hall for music.

In the family activity, you'll create a model of your character, or that of a favorite Minecraft player, to place in your museum. Parents may want to create a custom skin for their character prior to beginning.

🧑‍🤝‍🧑 FAMILY ACTIVITY
Make a Foldable 3-D Paper Character

For this hands-on activity, everyone will be creating their own 3-D version of their character, or that of a favorite Minecraft personality, using the website *pixelpapercraft.com*.

⧗ APPROXIMATE TIME TO COMPLETE
1–2 hours

✂ MATERIALS
+ Access to a color printer
+ Scissors and glue
+ Minecraft username for each character you wish to recreate

1. Visit *pixelpapercraft.com* and choose "Generators" from the menu options.

2. Under "Character Generators," choose "Minecraft Character," then select a "Skin." You'll see a deconstructed, printable image of your Minecraft character (A).

3. Print out the image and use scissors and glue to cut out and assemble the body parts (B).

4. Just for fun, you can also photocopy, cut out, and assemble the print version of one of our Minecraft characters.

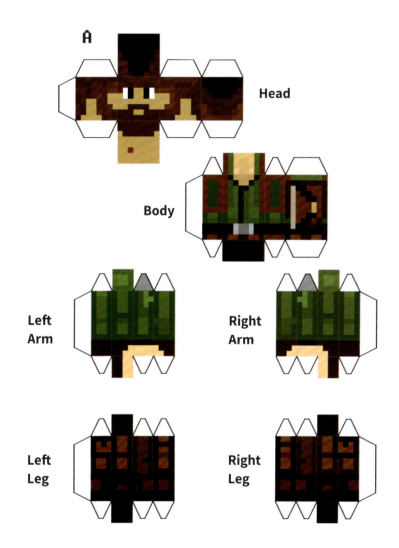

A

Head

Body

Left Arm

Right Arm

Left Leg

Right Leg

B

Design a Museum and Sculpt a Masterpiece

Your challenge is in two parts. First, design the layout for a museum with indoor and outdoor space where you can display your creations. Second, sculpt your character on top of a pedestal for all to admire.

1. Plan and then build the museum space and the pedestals you'll use to display your completed statues. Graph paper will be useful to designate areas of the museum.

2. Locate a suitable biome in your Minecraft world that works best with your design. Perhaps your museum might hover in the sky or float on the ocean. Consider the location of the rising and setting sun, water features, and especially pretty views before building. Flatten out any area that needs it, lay out your floor plan, and build your pedestals (B). You'll need an 8 x 4 space to support the legs.

✎ **GAME MODE**
Creative

⌛ **APPROXIMATE TIME TO COMPLETE**
2–3 hours

SHARE YOUR WORK

Share this lab online or in print by creating a collage combining images taken of your 3-D characters with your Minecraft build. Be sure to include multiple angles and images of your work taken at night and caption each image.

A

3. Determine the size of each sculpture based on skill level. Beginners may wish to sculpt a bust of the head while more advanced players should recreate the entire body.

4. Use the 3-D character you created in the family activity as a model and prepare your palette with appropriate colors and textures. Choose blocks that closely match your character and add them to your toolbar and backpack for quick access (C).

5. Sculpt your character from the ground up to eliminate mistakes later (D).

6. Add lighting (glowstone) to illuminate your masterpiece at night (E). Create walkways and viewing platforms between each sculpture.

B

C

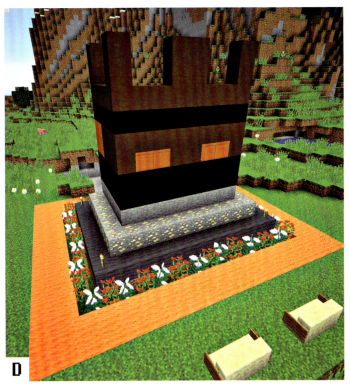

D

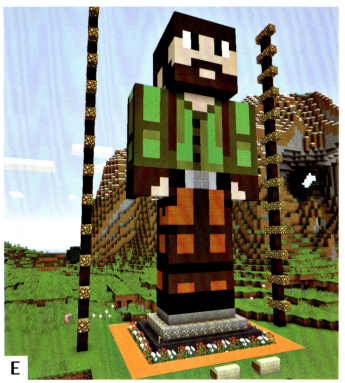

E

Setting the Stage

In this lab, you'll first recreate a favorite scene from a book or story using Minecraft shadow puppets in the family activity. Then you'll take what you've learned and recreate that same scene or a new one inside your Minecraft museum. It's a chance for the whole family to perform under the bright glowstone lights on stage!

FIND IT ONLINE

+ Read about the legend of *The Butterfly Lovers* here: *bit.ly/4cDgO9g*.

+ For help making a shadow puppet, watch this video created by a professional puppeteer: *bit.ly/3W4NIIG*.

Shadow Puppets

To begin this lab, you'll make shadow puppets and perform a scene from a favorite story. Shadow plays have a long tradition in China and Southeast Asia. We were inspired by the traditional Chinese story of *The Butterfly Lovers*, considered to be one of China's great folktales. Like Shakespeare's *Romeo and Juliet*, the legend of *The Butterfly Lovers* is about two tragic lovers.

⧗ APPROXIMATE TIME TO COMPLETE

1–2 hours

✄ MATERIALS

+ A short story with enough characters for each family member
+ Construction paper in a dark color, such as black or brown
+ Scissors
+ Tape
+ Long sticks
+ Focused light source, such as a small spot lamp or bright flashlight

A

1. Everyone will create a character from the scene you've selected. Sketch the outline of the character on the black construction paper. Use Minecraft-inspired mobs and characters, or create original puppets to tell your story. We created butterflies to represent our characters (A). See page 134 for a full-size template.

2. Cut out each character and tape it to the long stick to make it come alive (B).

B

3. Traditionally, shadow plays involve a thin, light-colored fabric on which the puppeteers project their puppets' shadows from behind. You'll need to hang a sheet if you wish to perform your play this way; otherwise, you can project your story from the front onto a blank wall using a focused light source (C).

C

📇 MINECRAFT PLAY

Lights, Camera, Action

Using Minecraft to animate short stories is widely popular. Kids and adults are producing and sharing thousands of hours of original stories they create in Minecraft on YouTube. In this part of the lab, you'll take a scene from a story or movie that you like, build replica sets, write dialogue, perform, and record the scene before posting it on YouTube.

Before you start, take a few moments to watch the video by YouTuber Adam Clarke, a.k.a. Wizard Keen, called *When Stampy Came to Tea*, a retelling of the story *When Tiger Came to Tea* by Judith Kerr (see the link opposite).

1. Decide on a short scene to recreate. It should be under five minutes. Before filming any scenes of a movie, directors draw a quick and simple sketch of what they want each scene to look like using paper (A). A movie where the camera angle never changes can be boring. By changing the position of your camera, your viewers will get a different perspective of the action.

2. Now that you know what you need your set to look like, it's time to build it into your museum complex. Consider building it outdoors

✎ GAME MODE
Creative

⌛ APPROXIMATE TIME TO COMPLETE
2–3 hours

FIND IT ONLINE

+ Adam Clarke is a very talented Minecraft YouTuber. To see his movie *When Stampy Came to Tea,* check out this link: *bit.ly/4czXtpi.*

+ After Adam finished producing *When Stampy Came to Tea,* he wanted to share how he created the video in hopes of inspiring others to do the same. To learn how to tell a story using Minecraft, watch his video: *bit.ly/4f3un3e.*

A

MORE TO EXPLORE

For players looking for a bit more of a challenge, consider these options:

+ Film multiple scenes.

+ Design scenes that involve advanced redstone use.

+ Create an action adventure with special effects and TNT explosions.

and turning it into a proper theater, but not too far away from the music hall and sculpture garden (B). Dress the stage with items from your inventory. If you need help, check out the link found opposite to get a behind-the-scenes look at *When Stampy Came to Tea*.

B

3. Write the dialogue for each character in the scene and have each player practice reading aloud. Your script might look something like this:

- Villager: Have you been to our village before, Witch Claire? It seems I recognize you.
- Witch: Thank you for asking me to tea. Even though I have flown by often, I've never actually visited this village before.
- Villager: Perhaps we met somewhere else. Have you ever been to Mushroom Park near Middlebury? I am a regular visitor. I collect mushrooms there for my stew.

4. Rehearse the scene with all the actors and determine the camera angles you'll use (C).

5. It's time to film the scene (D). Dig yourself a hole and hop in it to get a more interesting camera angle. Refer to page 15 for tips on filming or screencasting your video.

6. When you've completed your video, it may need a bit of editing. If that's the case, you can edit it after you upload to your YouTube channel. Use the video editor (see page 13) to combine your scenes, add music and titles, and publish your masterpiece.

C

D

Construction Zone

To complete this quest, Minecrafters and their families will engineer solutions to various challenges.

Map Maker

In this lab, learn how to find north with a couple of sticks, and navigate back home in Minecraft.

WHAT'S THE SCIENCE?

The Sun's position in the sky can be used to determine east and west. By placing the first stick in the ground, a shadow is cast. While waiting for the shadow, the Earth is rotating on its axis. The tip of the shadow at the end of an hour creates the east-west line. Once east and west are known, north and south can be found at a 90-degree angle. As the Earth rotates on its axis, the Sun rises in the east and sets in the west.

GO BEYOND

+ Design and build a sundial clock.
+ Research why the Sun rises in the east and sets in the west.
+ Explore the shadow of Kukulkan at Chichen Itza, built by the Mayans, during an equinox.

Finding North

It's instinctual to want to know where we are in the world. Our devices know where we are using not only global positioning satellites (GPS) but also cell towers and Wi-Fi hotspots to approximate our location—but what happens when the battery runs out? Complete this lab and you'll always know how to find north, south, east, and west using a couple of easily gathered items.

⧗ APPROXIMATE TIME TO COMPLETE
1 hour

✂ MATERIALS
+ Two 1-yard (1 m) sticks
+ 2 rocks

1. Place one stick in the ground in an outdoor sunny spot. Set your first rock at the end of the shadow (A).

2. Wait at least 30 minutes (longer is better) and set the second rock at the end of the shadow (B).

3. Place the second stick in front of both rocks (C). Stand with your heels at the rocks facing away from the stick. You are facing north. Draw a line in the ground to mark north (D). This is also the basis of how a sundial clock works.

A

B

C

D

Map Maker

When roaming the wilds of Minecraft, we need to remember how to get back to our home and the cool places we discover. Minecraft has cardinal directions—north, south, east, and west—just as in real life. Coordinates play a key role in building our Minecraft maps. By using them, we can keep track of our finds while we explore and still make it back to our safe house before the mean mobs arrive.

1. On PC/Mac/Linux version of Minecraft, press the F3 key to launch the debug screen. Clouds move from east to west. The Sun rises in the east and sets in the west. Sunflowers always face east (A).

2. You can tell where the Sun and Moon are by crafting a clock. The hand on the clock points to the Sun or Moon, depending on whether it's day or night.

✎ **GAME MODE**
Creative

⌛ **APPROXIMATE TIME TO COMPLETE**
45 minutes

FIND IT ONLINE
Check out this video on coordinates from OMGcraft: *bit.ly/4cQcgMY.*

NOW TRY THIS
Craft Elytra wings and attempt to continuously fly to populate a map with maximum zoom.

A

3. In the debug screen on PC Minecraft, which shows in text format the player's map coordinates and other information, the cursor changes to a red, green, and blue axis pointer. Red points east, green points up, and blue points south. Jot down your coordinates. After you've written down your coordinates you can walk your way back. When walking east, your x-coordinate increases. When moving north, your z-coordinate decreases (B).

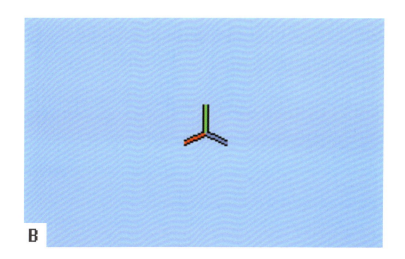

B

4. Craft a map and place it in your hand to reveal the surrounding terrain. Craft a zoomed-out map by placing paper around a crafted map. You can do this up to four times to craft a map that reveals over a four-million-block radius (C).

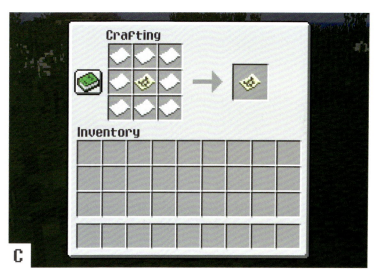

C

5. To obtain an explorer map, find a cartographer villager. Cartographers wear white clothing and trade emeralds for explorer maps (D). Note! Some villagers who wear white are librarians, not cartographers.

6. Trade with the cartographer until they give you an explorer map. You can get a woodland-explorer map that leads you to a huge woodland mansion or an ocean-monument explorer map that leads you to an underwater ocean mansion (see image on page 76). The woodland or ocean monument may be thousands of blocks away from your position. If you are off the map, you are a white dot. The map uses cardinal directions, so if the white dot is on the right-hand side of the map, you need to head west to find the monument.

D

Let There Be Light

Can you name all the colors found in a rainbow? How is a rainbow created? Let's discover the answer to both these questions by creating a colorful light spectrum, in-game using beacons. Out-of-game, create a gooey slime that glows in the dark!

STAY SAFE!
IMPORTANT NOTES FOR PARENTS AND KIDS:

+ Do *not* consume the goo! Although food ingredients are used to make it, it should *not* be eaten!

+ Parents should supervise this project, especially for young children. Make sure kids don't put their hands in their mouths when handling the ingredients.

+ This slime should be thrown out after one or two days.

WHAT'S THE SCIENCE?

The goo that you created exists in a very strange state. It feels like a solid and a liquid. When a substance behaves this way, scientists refer to it as a non-Newtonian fluid.

The paint contains a substance known as phosphors. Phosphors become energized by light and then slowly release that energy by glowing for several minutes afterward.

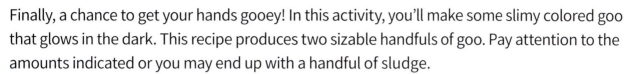

👥 FAMILY ACTIVITY

Glowing Goo

Finally, a chance to get your hands gooey! In this activity, you'll make some slimy colored goo that glows in the dark. This recipe produces two sizable handfuls of goo. Pay attention to the amounts indicated or you may end up with a handful of sludge.

⧖ APPROXIMATE TIME TO COMPLETE
15 minutes + at least 1 hour to charge the glow-in-the-dark paint

✂ MATERIALS
+ Mixing bowl
+ Spatula (optional)
+ 1½ cups (350 ml) marshmallow creme (such as Marshmallow Fluff) or melted marshmallows
+ 1½ cups (350 ml) cornstarch
+ 2 ounces (50 ml) glow-in-the-dark craft acrylic paint
+ Bright light source

1. In a mixing bowl, combine the marshmallow creme or melted marshmallows and 1 cup (235 ml) of the cornstarch. Use your hands or a spatula to mix until a soft dough-like goo forms (A).

2. Add the paint to the goo, drizzling in a little at a time (B). Fold the paint into the goo until fully blended. If the goo is too sticky, add more cornstarch.

3. The goo needs to be placed near a bright, consistent light source for an hour or more to fully charge (C).

4. After sufficient time has passed to charge the goo, it's time to turn off the lights (D)!

A

B

C

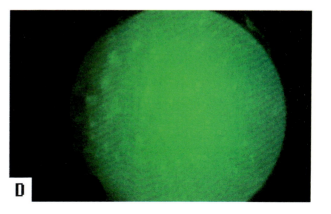

D

Construct Spectrum Beacons

Minecraft beacons are used to shine a bright light high into the sky, which provides players a landmark to return to. In survival mode, they can also affect nearby players in numerous ways.

In this activity, you'll place seven beacons in a row and use colored glass to create a spectrum, which includes the colors of the rainbow. You'll want to assemble your beacon tower near the laboratory you created in Lab 5, preferably on top of a hill or mountain.

1. Beacons are found in your creative inventory. In order for them to work, you will need to place them in the center and on top of a pyramid of metal blocks: iron, gold, diamond, or emerald. The simplest pyramid is made on one level in a 3 × 3 pattern, while the most complicated one is created with a 9 × 9 base and has four levels (A).

2. Construct the bases for seven 3 × 3 pyramids adjacent to each other. You don't need any space between each pyramid base, so the foundation will be 7 × 3 blocks. Place your beacons in the center of each 3 × 3 section, and beacons must be evenly distributed (B). Tip: If your game has cheats enabled, you can turn day into night by typing in the following command: /time set night.

GAME MODE
Creative

⏳ APPROXIMATE TIME TO COMPLETE
1 hour

NOW TRY THIS
Pistons cannot move beacons directly, but they can move other blocks. Experiment and determine a way to use pistons, redstone, and daylight sensors to activate each of your beacons when night falls. Experiment with mixing colors of stained glass. What happens if you place a light blue stained glass block on top of a yellow block?

A

3. Look carefully at the illustration of the rainbow (C). Its colors are arranged in a specific order. Starting from the left, what are they? Scientists use a memory trick to remember the order of the colors. Remember the name, Roy G. Biv, where R is red, O is orange, Y is yellow, G is green, B is blue, I is indigo, and V is violet. It turns out that Minecraft includes blocks representing each of these colors. Open your creative inventory and first find, then hold down the shift key and right-click to place, these stained-glass blocks on top of each beacon in the correct order (D):

- Red stained glass
- Orange stained glass
- Yellow stained glass
- Green stained glass
- Light blue stained glass
- Blue stained glass (very close to the color indigo)
- Purple stained glass

4. Time to make an even bolder statement. Remember the name? Locate the corresponding wool blocks in your inventory and cover up each pyramid (E).

5. Fly back to your laboratory and take a look. Is Roy G. Biv shining brightly in the night sky (see image on page 80)? Scientists have discovered that light we see as white is actually a combination of all the colors of the rainbow.

FIND IT ONLINE

Here's a link to an impressive beacon tower created by YouTuber CR3W, who figured out how to use redstone mechanisms and circuitry to simulate a beautiful rainbow beacon: *bit.ly/3XXL9uv.*

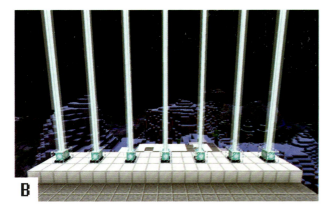

B

C

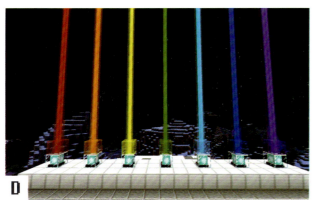

D

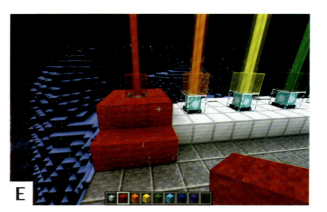

E

Crystals

This lab is all about crystals: how they form, the shapes they take, and how they fit together. In the hands-on activity, you'll create colorful crystals out of laundry detergent. In the Minecraft challenge, you'll build a giant crystal castle using ice, quartz, diamonds, and emeralds.

WHAT'S THE SCIENCE?

Epsom salt contains the chemical magnesium sulfate and forms a crystal structure. When it is mixed with warm water, the structure breaks down. As the solution cools, the atoms reform into another crystal structure.

FIND IT ONLINE

We love this video that demonstrates how ice crystals are formed in mineral water: *bit.ly/4d24HCt.*

FAMILY ACTIVITY
Make Your Own Crystals

⌛ APPROXIMATE TIME TO COMPLETE
1 hour, plus time for crystals to form

✂ MATERIALS
+ Epsom salt, in a 1:1 ratio with water (we used 8 ounces/236.6 ml water to 1 cup/250 ml salt crystals)
+ 2 or 3 wide-mouth, deep jars or drinking glasses
+ Food coloring (optional)
+ Warm water
+ Stirring sticks
+ Scissors (optional)
+ Several white ¼-inch (6 mm) pipe cleaners
+ Several blue ¼-inch (6 mm) pipe cleaners (optional)
+ String or fishing line
+ Pencils

In this lab, you'll witness how crystals grow and take the shape of a beautifully colored snowflake.

1. Gather your materials (A). Pour Epsom salt solution into each jar. Add food coloring, if desired. Pour warm tap water into each jar and stir rapidly until the crystals are completely dissolved. You want to create a super-saturated solution, which means crystals remain at the bottom even after vigorous stirring.

2. Cut or twist the pipe cleaners down to size, as needed to fit into your jars. Twist them into the shape of random snowflakes, and suspend them in each jar using string and a pencil (B).

3. Place the jars in a safe location, or in the refrigerator, where they will not be disturbed. Within 24 hours, you should have a healthy colony of crystals developing on your snowflakes (C). Remove from the solution when you are satisfied and hang in a bright place to catch the light (D).

A

B

C

D

Build a Crystal Castle

You may want to call in lots of family and friends for this activity. The challenge is to build a sizable castle in a cold biome out of giant crystals of various shapes. You should use mostly ice, both packed ice and regular ice, but diamonds, emeralds, and quartz are crystals, too, so use a few of those, as well. We'll show you what each type of crystal would look like if built in Minecraft, then it's your challenge to create a castle using as many of the crystal shapes as you can.

1. Pick a location in a cold biome. Bonus if there are already ice spikes growing (A).

2. Cubic crystal: This is the easiest and provides the most options. Make your cubic crystals with six, eight, or twelve sides. They can be made of ice or diamonds (B).

3. Hexagonal crystal: These have a familiar shape for Minecraft players. They can be made of ice, emerald, or quartz blocks (C). The hexagon shape would be excellent for tall towers.

4. Monoclinic crystal: These strange shapes look like a box that is about to fall over. These should be made of ice (D).

5. Orthorhombic crystal: Attach two Minecraft pyramids together at their bases (E).

6. Tetragonal crystal: Stretch out a cube and attach a pyramid on either end. These should be made of ice (F).

✎ **GAME MODE**
Creative

⧗ **APPROXIMATE TIME TO COMPLETE**
2-3 hours

A

B

C

7. Triclinic crystal: Just about anything goes with these. They tend to be flatter than the others and have multiple sides (G).

8. Build your castle out of an assortment of crystal shapes. Some can be standing up, others lying down. Set a few on their edges and some should lie flat. Add lighting, but be careful with torches and lava near ice. Packed ice won't melt, but regular ice will and make quite a mess. Put in stairs, ladders, doors, and windows to suit your taste.

9. Refer to the image on page 84 to see how we built our castle out of giant crystals.

NOW TRY THIS
+ We added a bit of lava to our castle. Modify this build to make it a fire and ice castle.
+ Turn this build into a fun parkour map. Sliding on ice can make it much more difficult.

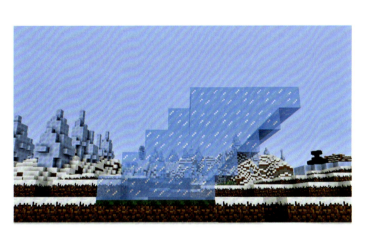

D

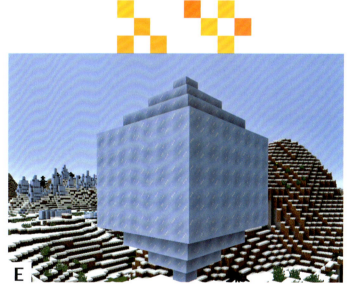

E

F

G

Catch a Wave

Waves aren't limited to water crashing at the beach. Actually, waves are all around us. For instance, the colors we see with our eyes have traveled in visible color waves, and the signal on your cell phone travels in radio waves.

In this lab, you'll study waves in a homemade wave pool and build a water dam inside Minecraft. There are a few key terms to understand before we dive into waves: crest, trough, wavelength, amplitude, and frequency (see "What's the Science?" at right).

Special tools are required to study the invisible radio waves that surround us every day. On the other hand, using a few household materials will enable you to create and study water waves.

WHAT'S THE SCIENCE?

The high point of a wave is the *crest*, or peak, while its low point is the *trough*. Whenever there's a disturbance (such as wind), the response is typically a wave traveling outward. As the waves get closer to shore, they create breaking waves, which are affected by the shape of the beach. *Wavelength* is the distance between the high points of a wave. *Amplitude* is the height of the peak or the depth of the trough from the baseline. *Frequency* is the amount of peaks and troughs in a given area in a second. To learn more about visible spectrum waves, check out Lab 14 (see page 80).

🙎 FAMILY ACTIVITY
Build a Wave Pool

⧗ APPROXIMATE TIME TO COMPLETE
45 minutes

✂ MATERIALS
+ Baking pan
+ Sand
+ Water
+ Ruler

1. Use a deep-walled baking pan to help prevent water from spilling over the sides. Place the baking pan on a level surface (A).

2. Spread sufficient sand on one side of the pan to create a small artificial beach. Pour water to create a pool approximately 2 inches (5 cm) deep (B). Add water to the pan slowly to prevent beach erosion. Reshape the sand beach to one side of the pan, if needed. Let the water settle and measure the water depth.

3. One person should hold the ruler along the side of the pan while the other creates waves. Use the palm of your hand to push into the water. Measure the crest and valley of the waves. Try different types of hand positions as well as stronger or lighter force (C). What do you notice? Using a camera to record the waves makes it easier to see the crest and valley of the waves.

4. Create a different base for the waves by adding sand to the other side of the pan. Shape the sand under the water to explore new wave forms (D).

A

B

C

D

💻 MINECRAFT PLAY

Construct a Dam

Although there are no waves in Minecraft, we can use our imagination with the unique characteristics of water, in-game, while building a dam. Dams are built to retain only a certain amount of water and to release excess water through spillways or floodgates. When it rains and the water level behind the dam rises, the floodgates open to release water. Ungated dams have spillways that allow water to spill over a specific height of the dam.

1. Explore a creative world to find a worthy canyon in a Mesa biome (A). See Find It Online, on page 91, for a link to find specific biomes. If you can't find a Mesa biome, try an amplified biome or a plains biome.

2. Use the unique features of water to your advantage. Start by filling the canyon with water. A trick is to build a layer of dirt the level you want the water. Pour lots of water buckets on top of the dirt (B).

3. Where the water cascade ends, start building the dam. Dams typically angle back toward the water. The lowest level is stepped away from the water, while the second and third levels are tiered back toward the water.

4. Finish the third layer of the dam one block below the water level. Top the dam with cobblestone wall and mossy cobblestone wall. You should have a dam built to the water level with three tiered levels (C). Switch between the three types of blocks for a naturally weathered-looking dam.

✎ GAME MODE
Creative

⧗ APPROXIMATE TIME TO COMPLETE
45 minutes

A

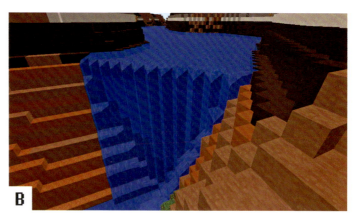

B

C

5. To build the redstone dam gates, create a corridor behind the dam. Redstone breaks when it gets wet, so be sure to craft a dry area for all your redstone items (D). In our example, the redstone build area is below the water level behind the dam. Look carefully to see water dripping from the ceiling.

6. Break an area large enough in the front of the dam to add sticky piston gates. Add sticky pistons and build a small water source to release the water when the pistons are deactivated. Place a stone block on the end of the sticky pistons to blend in with the dam (E).

7. Place a lever in a convenient location to activate/deactivate the sticky pistons. Tunnel to the side of the dam, and place redstone dust and repeaters to reach the lever. Flip the lever to release the flood down the dam and into the river (F). Our example shows the finished dam.

FIND IT ONLINE
+ Use this link to find specific biomes: *bit.ly/46oazUA*.
+ Check out HermitCraft's dam, which operates based on sunlight: *bit.ly/3WiYMDp*.

D

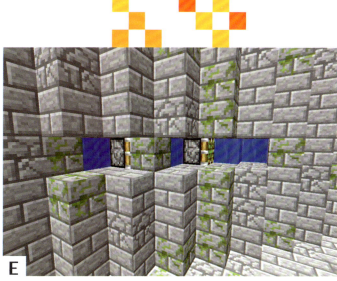

E

F

NOW TRY THIS
+ Craft a working dam that automatically waters crops.
+ Build a Kundt's tube, a device used by scientists, to demonstrate standing waves: *bit.ly/3Wp0QIR*.
+ Research and build an oscilloscope in Minecraft using repeaters.

Cycles in Science

To complete this quest, Minecrafters and their families will explore cycles in science.

Egg Farm

One thing you've got to love about Minecraft: chickens! Any Minecraft player will tell you that chickens are a wonderful source of meat and eggs, but my goodness—they can be so annoying. We decided to give them their own spotlight in this lab. You'll learn how to automate an egg ranch in Minecraft and participate in a fun engineering competition with family and friends.

WHAT'S THE SCIENCE?

Look in your refrigerator or at a package that a delivery driver brings you and see how the product is packaged. What materials or precautions did the shipper or manufacturer include to keep the product safe or fresh? Scientists help develop inexpensive, lightweight, and recyclable packaging materials that will allow even the most fragile of objects to be shipped around the world with the smallest amount of waste. Egg containers are usually made from cardboard or a foam-like material. Why?

FAMILY ACTIVITY
Egg Drop Challenge

The egg drop challenge is upon you. There are several options for completing this lab, so select the one that works best for you. The goal of each is to engineer a container that will keep an egg from breaking, despite being dropped from a predetermined height.

⧗ APPROXIMATE TIME TO COMPLETE
1 hour

✄ MATERIALS
+ Eggs
+ Utility tape
+ Containers
+ Various packing material
+ You will also need a location, such as a second-story balcony, from which to drop your containers. If that is not possible, each container can be tossed or launched into the air from ground level.

A

B

Option 1: Materials
With this option, limit all engineers to the same set of materials (A). Engineers can use only the materials given, but may assemble their package in any way they wish.

Option 2: Containers
Give each participant the same container, such as take-out boxes, Styrofoam cups, or recyclable plant containers, but let them choose packing materials from a large pile of options. Another variation of this option is to toss a "secret ingredient" into the mix, something that everyone must use.

Option 3: Math Game
Each item used has a value, or imaginary cost, associated with it. The goal is to see who can keep an egg safe at the lowest cost of materials (B). Items like bubble wrap and cotton should cost much more than tape.

Option 4: Mass
If you have access to a digital scale, you will be able to determine the mass of each container. Mass indicates the amount of matter in the container. Who can design a container that has the lowest mass and keeps an egg from breaking?

Option 5: Size
What is the smallest container you can design to save the egg? Use a measuring tape around the widest location to determine a winner.

Automated Egg Collector

What would you do with all the cake and pumpkin pie you could eat? Well, you'll need dozens of eggs, so let's get busy building a chicken coop that collects eggs for you automatically. Build it near your laboratory, but not too near because these chickens will be making a lot of noise!

1. Build a 7 × 7 foundation slab using the block of your choice (A).

2. Build an exterior wall all the way around, leaving a spot for a door. Attach six hoppers to the back of six trapped chests (B).

3. To attach a hopper to the back of a trapped chest, hold down the shift key while right-clicking with the hopper in your hand (C).

4. Extend the walls to the inside and add iron bars across the length of both sides of the coop (D).

✐ GAME MODE
Creative or survival

⧗ APPROXIMATE TIME TO COMPLETE
1 hour

FIND IT ONLINE
Of course, chickens are a good source of meat, as well. Check out this redstone-powered automated chicken farm: *bit.ly/4bFtiMm.*

A

5. With a chicken spawn egg (or regular egg) in your hand, right-click inside the hopper to place a chicken in it. Quickly place one more wood plank block on the roof to trap the chicken inside (E).

6. Check each morning and you should discover a fresh supply of eggs inside the chests.

NOW TRY THIS

+ Need a lot of eggs? See how many chickens you can get into each hopper.

+ Now that you've automated egg collection, design a way to harvest wheat.

+ Create an entire working farm filled with animals and vegetables.

B

C

D

E

Build a Battery

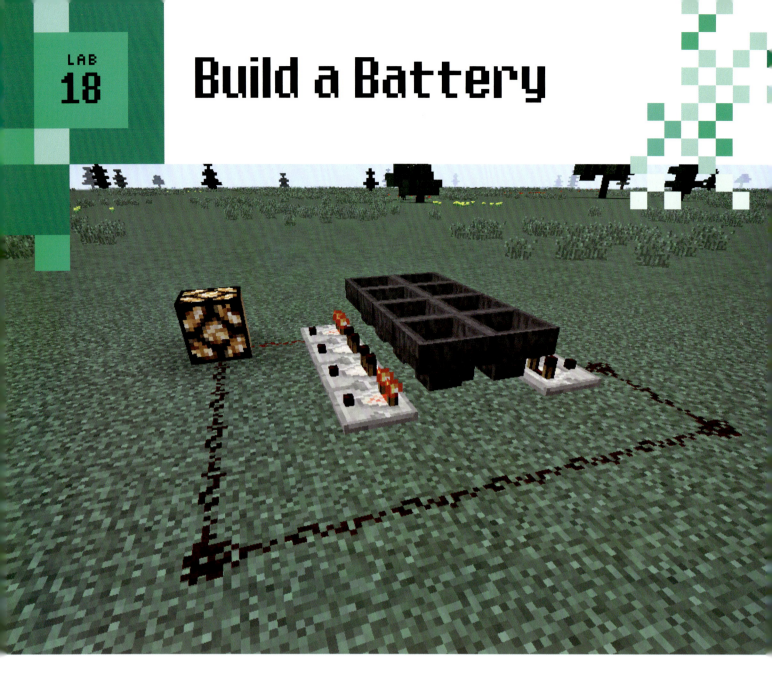

Batteries are used in nearly all the electronic equipment we interact with daily. From cell phones to video game controllers, batteries have the important job of supplying portable electricity. Batteries supply electricity through a chemical reaction that creates electrical energy. By recharging rechargeable batteries, we reverse the process to resupply electrical energy.

For the in-game section of the lab, you'll build a hopper pipe that simulates the flow of electrons within a battery. In the family activity, you'll build a battery with some pennies, foil, cardboard, and vinegar. Increase the voltage of your battery by adding more layers (cells).

After building this simple battery, you may just have a newfound appreciation for batteries you encounter daily.

FAMILY ACTIVITY
Build a Battery

⏳ APPROXIMATE TIME TO COMPLETE
30 minutes

✂ MATERIALS
+ Pennies
+ Pencil
+ Cardboard from a cereal or tissue box
+ Scissors
+ Foil
+ Bowl
+ White vinegar
+ Tape
+ Small LED or multimeter

FIND IT ONLINE

This TED Ed video does a great job explaining how batteries work: *bit.ly/4d690g4.*

1. Gather your materials. You'll need coin-size circles of cardboard. Trace one of the pennies on the cardboard at least ten times to create a template for cutting (A). Note: You'll find thin cardboard in cereal and tissue boxes. Cut out the circles carefully. If they are too large the edges of the cardboard will make the battery less efficient.

2. This battery uses the chemical properties of dissimilar metals to transfer energy. In addition to copper, the battery uses aluminum foil. You'll need about ten pieces of foil. Fold the foil four times. Trace a coin and cut out the shapes (B). Carefully separate the foil layers. Tip: Wet one fingertip to grab each thin layer of foil.

(continued)

A

B

FAMILY ACTIVITY

3. Place the ten pieces of cardboard into a small bowl. Pour enough white vinegar to cover each cardboard piece. Allow the cardboard to absorb the vinegar; this may take over a minute (C). The cardboard needs time to absorb the liquid to allow the electrons to pass through the cells.

4. Stack your battery in this order: coin, foil, vinegar-soaked cardboard, coin, foil, vinegar-soaked cardboard (D). Stack at least eight layers. Begin and end the battery with a coin. Wrap tape around the stacked battery to help it stay together. Each layer is a battery cell. Add more cells to add more energy.

5. Connect a small LED or multimeter to your battery to measure the voltage (E). If the voltage seems especially low, check the connections between the layers. AA and AAA batteries produce 1.5 volts, and a 9-volt battery produces 9 volts.

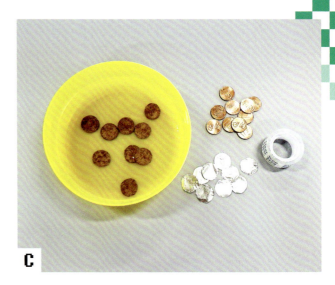

C

D

GO BEYOND

What happens when you add or take away cells of your battery? What other materials can you use to make a battery?

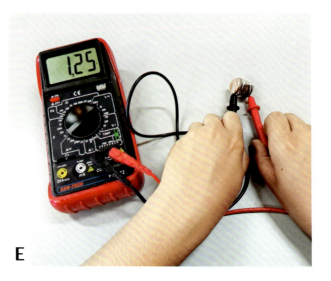

E

Hopper Battery

Hoppers are clever items to help automate your work. When we drop an item into one of the hoppers, it is transferred like the chemicals in a physical battery around a circuit.

1. Craft or collect at least eight hoppers, eight redstone comparators, and an item of your choice.

2. Place the first hopper in a space with room for seven more. The consecutive hoppers must be attached to the first by holding shift on the PC. The hopper pipe must be like a circuit with one hopper connected to the next (A).

(continued)

✎ GAME MODE
Creative

⧗ APPROXIMATE TIME TO COMPLETE
25 minutes

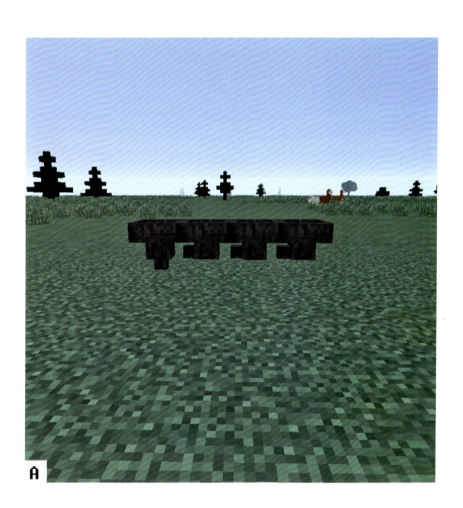

A

3. Break the first hopper and replace it by holding shift and your place button. This will make a complete circuit and determine whether the hopper pipe continues circulating the item (B).

4. Stand on top of the hopper and place a comparator pointing away from the hopper. The comparators will become a visual to see what happens as the item travels around the circuit. Drop any item into one of the hoppers. Watch it move from one hopper to the next, lighting a comparator as it circulates (C).

5. If your item doesn't circulate, go back to steps 2 and 3 to make sure your hoppers are connected in the pipe form. The lower part of the hopper must be curved.

6. For added visual effect, place redstone dust and a lamp down from one end of your hopper pipe to the other. Although this isn't improving your hopper pipe, it appears to look more like a complete circuit with battery, wires, and light (see photo page 98).

NOW TRY THIS

+ Your hopper pipe is a slow redstone clock. Try adding it to your Chain Reaction Contraption in Lab 22 (page 120).

+ This build would work great with the Zombie Dance Party in Lab 2 on page 26.

B

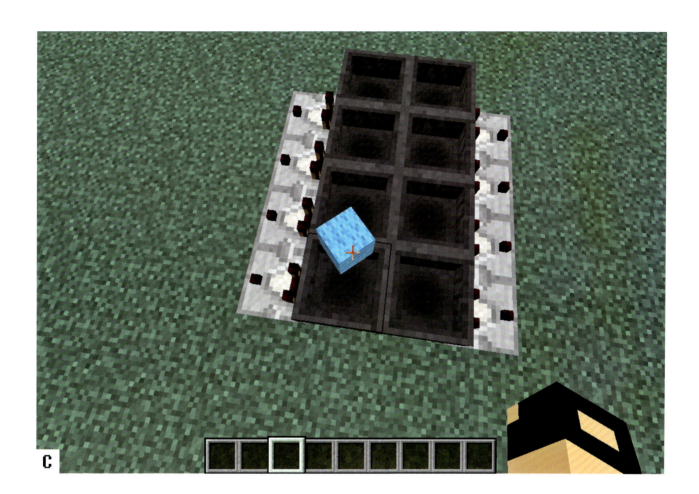

WHAT'S THE SCIENCE?

The battery you created has three parts: an anode, a cathode, and the electrolyte. Each three-part layer—coin, foil, cardboard—makes one battery cell. The positive terminal is the cathode, while the negative is the anode, and the electrolyte allows the chemical reaction inside the battery to initiate the flow of electrons to travel from anode (negative) to cathode (positive). The anode releases the electron while the cathode accepts the electron. Once the battery is connected with some resistance, like a lightbulb or the multimeter, the circuit is closed. As the electrons flow around the circuit, the light illuminates or the multimeter displays the energy produced. The design of your battery is built on the Voltaic pile battery by Alessandro Volta (1745—1827), which he devised in 1800. The copper and aluminum pieces are electrodes while the vinegar is the electrolyte. The electrolyte increases conductivity, which increases your battery's voltage.

Create an Ecosystem

Terrariums allow the opportunity to grow plants in different climates. If you live in a dry, desert-like climate, you can grow humidity-loving tropical plants in a closed terrarium, which creates its own environment that is more humid than the ambient air in your house.

In the hands-on activity, you'll create a closed terrarium that not only nourishes plants with nutrients from soil but also recycles water through the water cycle. In the game activity, you'll replicate a terrarium near your science laboratory.

A

B

👪 FAMILY ACTIVITY

Terrarium

Tropical plants like ferns, Fittonia, baby's tears, Pilea, begonia, Cryptanthus, oak leaf creeping fig, and small palm trees work great in a closed terrarium. Terrariums make great gifts because they require little care and look great. Building one with a large clear and empty soda bottle is a great way to upcycle. Take care when adding the layers to your terrarium.

⏳ APPROXIMATE TIME TO COMPLETE
45 minutes

✂ MATERIALS
+ Rubber band
+ Plastic drink bottle (2L)
+ Ruler
+ Marker
+ Scissors
+ Sand
+ Small rocks
+ Activated charcoal
+ Sphagnum moss
+ Potting soil
+ Small moisture-loving plant of your choice (see suggestions above)
+ Clear packing tape

1. Gather the materials (A).

2. Stretch a rubber band around the bottle about 4 inches (10 cm) above the bottom. Draw a line on the bottle above the band (B). Remove the rubber band and cut along the line.

3. Layer 1 inch (2.5 cm) of sand, 1 inch (2.5 cm) of small rocks, and ½ inch (1.3 cm) of activated charcoal (C). The charcoal has tiny openings that grab impurities in the water, like a water filter you might use at home.

4. Add a thin layer of moist sphagnum moss, and 2 inches (5 cm) of damp potting soil (wet the moss and potting soil before adding them to the terrarium). Add your small plant (D).

5. Place the upper section of the bottle on top. Use tape to seal (E). Twist off the cap to add water or allow excess water to evaporate. Learn from our mistake: too much light will burn the plants.

C

D

E

Closed Terrarium

The Jungle biome is most closely related to a real-life humid environment. Inside the Minecraft terrarium, create a small version of the Jungle biome. Build the terrarium above ground using clear glass blocks and the layers of soil to replicate a real terrarium in life.

1. Select a location near your science laboratory or field station. Build your terrarium in a biome that is drier than the Jungle biome to provide a contrast between dry and humid environments.

2. Plan your bottle shape. Build a 6 × 6 base layer of glass with cobblestone surrounding it. Break the corner blocks to make the base look like a rounded bottle shape (A).

3. Build the lower half of the terrarium by crafting nine levels of glass following your base layer pattern. Leave a side section exposed for greater access to the layers of soil (B).

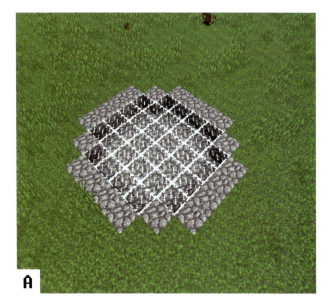

A

✏ GAME MODE
Creative

⧖ APPROXIMATE TIME TO COMPLETE
25 minutes

GO BEYOND

If you love plants, look into becoming a horticulturist or landscape architect.

NOW TRY THIS

Connect your terrarium with your science laboratory, but be sure to set up a method of sealing your terrarium to keep the water cycle in a closed loop.

PLANTS
Tall grass
Vines
Ferns
Jungle wood and leaves
Oak wood and leaves
Dandelion flowers
Cocoa beans
Poppy flowers
Melons

MOBS	
Passive Mobs:	**Hostile Mobs:**
Ocelots	Spiders
Chickens	Endermen
Cows	Witches
Sheep	Skeletons
Pigs	Creepers
Parrots	Zombies
Villagers	

4. The base layer of the terrarium needs to be sand. On top of the sand, add a layer of cobblestone. Both the stone and the sand act as filters for the water as it drains through the soil. On top of the cobblestone, add a layer of coal blocks. Just like in our family activity, the coal acts like a scrubber for the water, adding greater purification as it is recycled in the terrarium (C). This is similar to how water is purified in real life as it leaches through layers of earth to the water table below.

5. Add one layer of jungle leaves to simulate sphagnum moss. The moss adds a layer of moisture to help your plant self-water. Add dirt blocks to fill in the top three layers.

6. Build a jungle tree out of jungle wood and leaf blocks to simulate a growing tree. Jungle saplings will only grow if you have a terrarium with plenty of room. If you want to grow plants from seeds, try adding smaller plants found in the Jungle biome like melons, ferns, and flowers (D).

7. Craft the top section of the terrarium to resemble a bottle. Double the base nine layers to craft the top half of the bottle, depending on the types of plants planted. Consider adding a couple of passive mobs inside your terrarium. Add a cap at the top to make it more visually similar to a bottle (E). Use red wool or concrete to give that just-capped look.

B

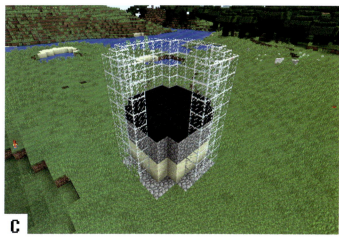

C

D

E

Quantum Physics

GRASSLAND Field Station　MESA Field Station　MARINE Field Station　ANTARCTIC Field Station　DESERT Field Station　MOUNTAIN Field Station

It's time to think about the very small and learn how scientists believe information is transported across great distances very quickly. You'll begin by examining 3-D movie glasses, up close, and uncover how our brain makes sense of what we see. In Minecraft, you'll learn about the science around a concept known as quantum teleportation. You'll use command blocks to set up teleport stations that allow digital visitors to move quickly around your STEM world.

FIND IT ONLINE

You can view images of what the surface of Mars looks like by visiting the NASA site, below, and wearing your 3-D glasses. How do you think the robot was able to take these photos? *go.nasa.gov/3SscNfT.*

🧑‍🤝‍🧑 FAMILY ACTIVITY

Shifting Perspectives

In this lab, you will look at the world through 3-D movie glasses, learn how a stereoscopic image is formed, and examine the role color plays in our lives.

⌛ APPROXIMATE TIME TO COMPLETE
1 hour

✂ MATERIALS
+ Red-and-blue 3-D glasses, one for each family member, plus one additional pair
+ A mirror
+ Scissors

A

1. Gather your materials (A). You can find 3-D red/blue glasses at novelty stores and online. All participants put on their glasses and face each other or look in the mirror. What do you notice with both eyes open about the other person? Now close one eye, then open it and close the other. What happens?

2. Cut one pair in half and cut off the part that goes around the ear (B). Lay one color on top of the other and look through the lens. What do you notice? Look up at the sky, but away from the Sun. What color is the sky? Can you explain why?

3. Look at the image of the planet Mars (C). It appears out of focus. Put on your 3D glasses and you'll see a 3-D image of the red planet. Other anaglyphs can be found online.

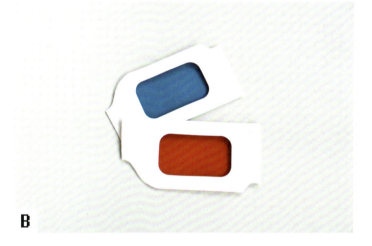

B

WHAT'S THE SCIENCE?

Our eyes gather information transmitted by light and our brain interprets it. Photons are the smallest unit of light and the information they transport is sometimes referred to as *quanta*. Red-and-blue glasses process two images taken by two different cameras slightly apart (just like our eyes) and merge them together to trick our brain. One camera has a blue filter on it and the other, a red filter.

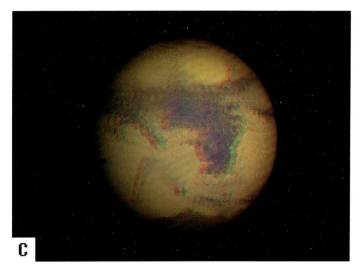

C

Quantum Teleporters

You designed and built a cool, automated laboratory in Lab 5 and have since created many additional field stations where you've been hard at work. Let's make it easier for your character to get to each work site by setting up command block teleporters.

In the world of physics, many scientists believe that information, like the exact location of your Minecraft character, can be transported over great distances very quickly. It's time to test that idea in Minecraft.

1. Command blocks cannot be found in the regular inventory, so players must summon one by typing in a command. For this to work, set the game settings to allow cheats, and you must play in creative mode. Type in the following command to summon a command block:

- /give @p minecraft:command_block. A command block like this one should pop into your inventory (A). In the Bedrock edition, use this command: /give @p command_block.

2. You will need to visit each of your field stations, stand in a comfortable spot, and record the coordinates. Begin with your science lab. Create a table like the one on page 111 to record the x, y, and z coordinates at each site. When you are standing in the correct location, press the F3 key and look for the three numbers just after xyz. They may look something like -2430 78 432.

A

GAME MODE
Creative

⏳ APPROXIMATE TIME TO COMPLETE
2 hours

FIND IT ONLINE
Did you have fun typing code into your command blocks? There are many more commands that can be issued with command blocks based on the version of the game you are playing. Try out the latest commands for each version by visiting the DigMinecraft site: *bit.ly/4foYKBg.*

GO BEYOND
There are two more versions in addition to command blocks. Chain command and repeating command blocks are set up in a similar way, but each can control a different aspect of the game. Visit the Minecraft Wiki and read about each block, then add one of each to your science lab: *bit.ly/4dDoLLR.*

3. Once you have all the coordinates you need, it's time to create your teleporter. Determine where you wish to place it in your lab. You will need as many command blocks as you have research stations. We placed our command blocks in the floor (B).

4. Right-click on top of each command block. In the box just below "Console Command," type the following:
- /tp @p x y z
- Replace the x, y, and z with the coordinates of the field station you wish to visit using this command block. Be sure to add a space after each coordinate. Click Done when you are finished.

5. Grab a button from your inventory and, while holding down the shift key, right-click on top of the command block to place it on the block (C). Your first command block teleporter is now ready to test! Click the button to see if you are transported to the field station.

6. Now that you are at your first field station, place another command block near the spot you just landed on. This time, dig a hole and place the command block inside. Right-click it and add the coordinates of your lab home base. Instead of a button, place a pressure plate on top of the command block by holding down the shift key before right-clicking (D).

7. Finish up by repeating steps 4 to 6 for each field station you wish to connect to your teleporter. To wrap it up and make it easier to identify each teleporter, place a sign behind each command block and type the name of the field station destination.

B

C

D

	Home Base	Desert Field Station	Mountain Field Station	Ocean Field Station	Polar Field Station
X					
Y					
Z					

Engineering Challenge

QUEST 6

To complete this quest, Minecrafters and their families will engineer solutions to several design challenges.

Code Your Commands

Programming has become increasingly important in our world. It takes programming to build and more programming to update Minecraft. Learn about programming while playing Minecraft!

WHAT'S THE SCIENCE?

Programming is the act of creating instructions in a specific language that a computer can compile and use. Computer science covers more than just programming; at its core, computer science is about solving problems. Computer scientists often become software engineers, people who work to build and repair software code.

FIND IT ONLINE

+ This video produced by Facebook (now Meta) explains the concept of computer science: *bit.ly/3Ltp8wc.*
+ Go to this web address for a printable version of our sample dot programming template: *bit.ly/3zYk8x1.*

Paper Coding Game

In this activity, you'll create a simple program so your partner can complete the dot programming game. A program is a list of instructions; this one tells your partner how to move through the game. The goal is to successfully move your partner through dot by dot, without running into any boundary lines. We created four designs that start off easy and gradually increase in difficulty.

⧖ APPROXIMATE TIME TO COMPLETE
1 hour

✄ MATERIALS
+ Dot programming sheet (see page 135)
+ Pencil
+ Paper

1. To complete the game, your partner will follow your instructions (program) to connect the dots. From the start position, write each move your partner will need to make from dot to dot. Choose from the following moves: draw right, draw left, draw up, draw down. If you'd like your partner to move in any direction more than one dot, you'll need to tell them. For example, to move up four dots, your program would read, "Draw up 4" (A).

2. The completed list of moves (commands) is your program. Give your program to your game partner and ask them to follow your moves exactly, even if it means not following the game boundary lines on the sheet. If your program crosses the game boundary lines or over itself, it's buggy. Debug your program by altering the moves (B).

3. You can create a program for one of the shapes shown in Image C, or draw your own design on dot paper (see page 135) and craft a program for your partner to follow.

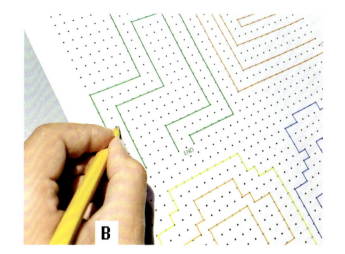

B

DRAW	UP 8
DRAW	RIGHT 7
DRAW	UP 8
DRAW	RIGHT 6
DRAW	DOWN 14
DRAW	LEFT 6

A

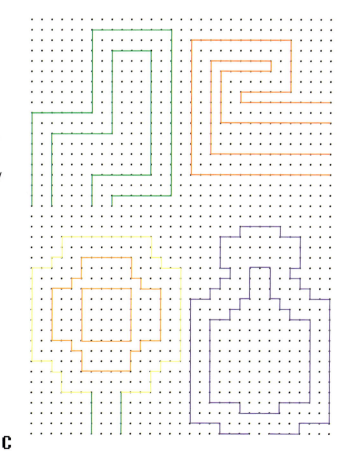

C

/Commands

For this in-game part of the lab, you'll type commands and get items that are impossible to collect in-game. Who doesn't want super-enchanted weapons? There are many more commands you can try in-game that are not covered in this lab. Try to figure out how to customize the commands as you work through the lab.

1. You must be OP (operator) in the world. In single player, either start the world with cheats on or open your world to LAN, press escape, and you'll see a button that says open to LAN. The commands must be typed in the chat box by pressing t or / to start a command (A).

2. Start with altering the weather and time of day. Type /weather thunder 100 and press enter. Type /set time night and press enter. There are three weather options: clear, rain, and thunder. The number at the end of the weather command is the number of ticks you're changing the weather.

3. Commands can be location specific. One of the most useful commands is the /tp command to teleport users around the world. Type /tp with coordinates to teleport yourself to a new location (B). An example is /tp 100 75 -270. When playing with others, teleport to them by typing /tp (person being teleported) (person at location). An example is /tp cscottsy escottsy (this command will send cscottsy to escottsy).

4. Many of the features you're used to are controlled by the command /gamerule. Turn inventory on and off by typing /gamerule keepInventory true (or false to turn it off).

5. With the /summon command, things get interesting. You can summon much more than a regular creeper or cow. With a few additions to a command or argument, you can change their characteristics. Type /summon and then press the space bar to see a list of options. Try summoning a cute frog or a tough armadillo! We summoned a chicken with a visible name, Cluck_cluck, one block above our coordinates (C).

6. Super-enchant a diamond sword by typing: /give @a minecraft:diamond_sword[minecraft: enchantments={levels:{'bane_of_arthropods':5,'fireaspect':2,'knockback':2,'looting':3, 'mending':1,'sharpness':5,'smite':3,'sweeping_edge':3,'unbreaking':3,'density':5,'wind_burst':3}}] This command will give you an enchanted diamond sword with bane of arthropods, fire aspect, knockback, looting, mending, sharpness, smite, sweeping edge, unbreaking, density, wind burst. Try it out on a Warden!

✎ **GAME MODE**
Creative or survival
(must be OP)

⏳ **APPROXIMATE TIME TO COMPLETE**
1 hour

FIND IT ONLINE
+ For a list of all the commands and how to use them, visit the Minecraft Wiki: *bit.ly/46mneag.*
+ Subscribe to slicedlime to learn more about how to make your own Minecraft commands: *bit.ly/46dlUGW.*

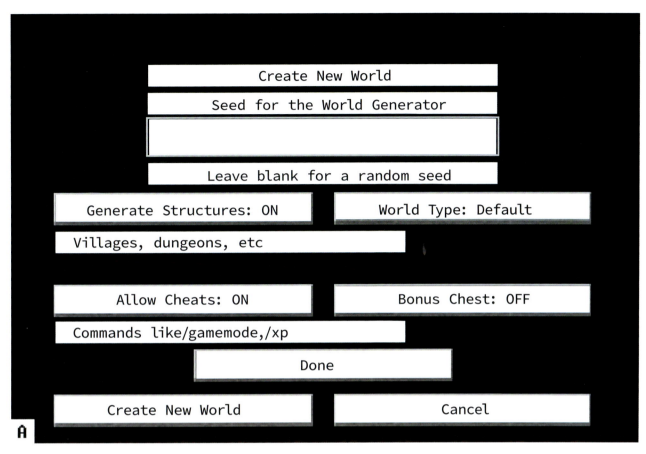

Create New World

Seed for the World Generator

Leave blank for a random seed

Generate Structures: ON   World Type: Default

Villages, dungeons, etc

Allow Cheats: ON   Bonus Chest: OFF

Commands like/gamemode,/xp

Done

Create New World   Cancel

A

B

C

Cluck_cluck

Cluck_cluck

Set the time to 1000 Object successfully summoned

/summon minecraft:chicken ~ ~1 ~ {CustomName:
"Cluck_cluck".CustomNameVisible:1}

(continued)

/Commands (continued)

Use this table as you craft your own enchanted tools. Don't forget to share super-powerful items with your friends.

ALL-PURPOSE ENCHANTMENTS	MAXIMUM ENCHANTMENT LEVEL
Mending	1
Unbreaking	3
Curse of Vanishing	1

ARMOR ENCHANTMENTS	MAXIMUM ENCHANTMENT LEVEL
Aqua Affinity	1
Blast Protection	4
Curse of Binding	1
Depth Strider	3
Feather Falling	4
Fire Protection	4
Frost Walker	2
Projectile Protection	4
Protection	4
Respiration	3
Soul Speed	3
Thorns	3
Swift Sneak	3

WEAPON ENCHANTMENTS	MAXIMUM ENCHANTMENT LEVEL
Bane of Arthropods	5
Efficiency	5
Fire Aspect	2
Looting	3
Impaling	5
Knockback	2
Sharpness	5
Smite	5
Sweeping Edge	3

BOW AND CROSSBOW ENCHANTMENTS	MAXIMUM ENCHANTMENT LEVEL
Channeling	1
Flame	1
Impaling	5
Infinity	1
Loyalty	3
Riptide	3
Multishot	1
Piercing	4
Power	5
Punch	2
Quick Charge	3

TOOL ENCHANTMENTS	MAXIMUM ENCHANTMENT LEVEL
Efficiency	5
Fortune (Increases certain item drop chances from blocks)	3
Luck of the Sea	3
Lure (Decreases wait time until fish/junk/loot "bites")	3
Silk Touch	1

Chain Reaction Contraption

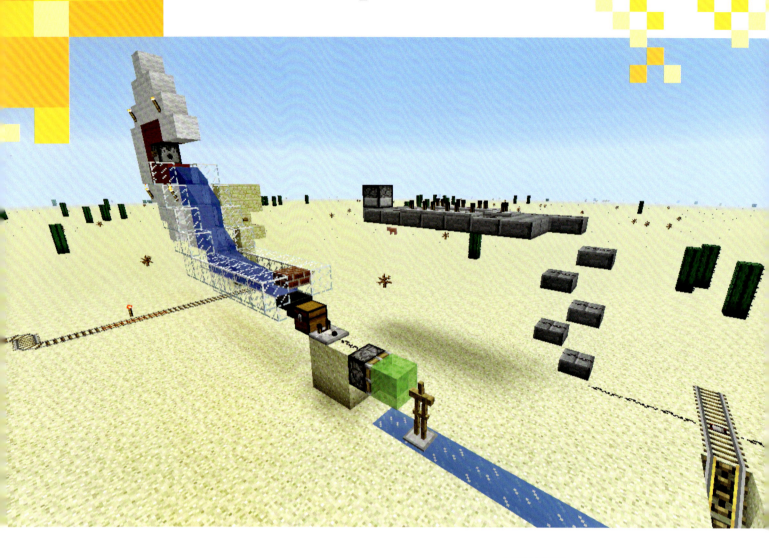

In this lab, you'll use simple mechanisms to create a chain reaction to accomplish a simple task, also known as Rube Goldberg machines. Consisting of mechanisms such as levers, pulleys, wheels and axles, screws, wedges, and gears, these machines are named after Rube Goldberg, a cartoonist and engineer who created famous newspaper cartoons. Some overly complex machines can take hours to build and seconds to perform. You'll get to build your own in and out of Minecraft.

FIND IT ONLINE

Learn more about Rube Goldberg, his comic strips, contests, and more: *rubegoldberg.org.*

Build a Rube Goldberg Machine

In this activity, we're going to build a Rube Goldberg machine. We pulled together a bunch of items lying around to build our example. The materials list is just a suggestion; see what you have around your house.

A

⧗ APPROXIMATE TIME TO COMPLETE

1 hour

✂ MATERIALS

+ Wooden train tracks with train
+ Dominoes
+ Large bouncy ball
+ Wood blocks
+ Books
+ Electrical surge protector with on/off switch
+ Electric fan

1. All great Rube Goldberg machines repurpose parts found around the house. While you design your machine, consider using old and new toys with string, tape, electrical switches, swinging bouncy balls, train tracks, balloons, and dominoes.

2. Every Rube Goldberg machine has a clever start. Try hanging a large bouncy ball taped on a string to create a pendulum. Pull back on the pendulum to kick-start your machine (A).

3. Our machine has six different reactions. A swinging ball hits the train that rolls into the dominoes. The dominoes hit the larger blocks, which hit the large wood train track pieces. The train track pieces fall onto the books, which tumble onto the electrical switch to turn on the fan (B).

4. It takes several tries to have one successful start-to-finish run (C). Don't worry if it takes dozens of attempts, as the best Rube Goldberg machines require a lot of patience.

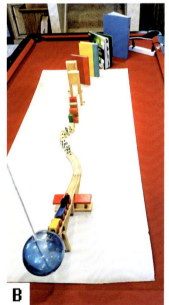

B

C

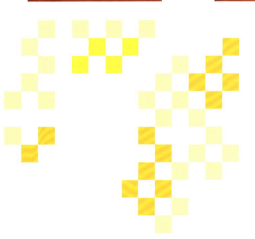

Rube Goldberg Meets Redstone

With a little creativity, you can use items in Minecraft to create reactions. Just as you built an actual machine in the family activity, you're going to design, build, test, and rebuild a Rube Goldberg machine in-game. You'll use dispensers, slime blocks, comparators, repeaters, pistons, detector rails, armor stands, and more!

1. Pick a fun location to craft your Rube Goldberg machine. Start and end your machine in a similar location. We've crafted a pumpkin pie delivery machine.

2. To start our Rube Goldberg chain reaction machine, we fire an arrow at a wooden button placed on the side of a dispenser. The dispenser releases a piece of redstone dust that flows down the river and into the chest (A).

3. At the end of the river, the redstone enters the hopper. The hopper moves the redstone into the chest. Once the chest has the redstone, the redstone comparator is activated (B).

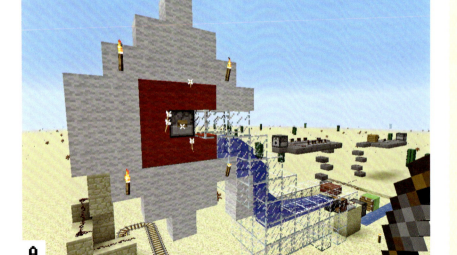

A

✏ GAME MODE
Creative

⧖ APPROXIMATE TIME TO COMPLETE
90 minutes

WHAT'S THE SCIENCE?

Using his training as an engineer and his sense of humor, Rube Goldberg (1883–1970) created comically complex machines to accomplish simple tasks, such as using a napkin or picking up soap that fell out of the bathtub. Rube Goldberg machines are a series of simple machines—lever, wheel and axle, pulley, inclined plane, wedge, and screw—which are the building blocks of more complex machines.

4. The redstone comparator sends a signal through redstone to activate the sticky piston. A slime block on the end of the sticky piston pushes the armor stand down the icy runway. The armor stand ends on a stone pressure plate (C). In this build, we're using a hopper to transfer the redstone dust collected from the end of the river into the chest.

5. The stone pressure plate sends a redstone signal to a powered redstone rail. Place a cart on top of the redstone rail. The block immediately behind the cart forces the cart to move once the redstone rail becomes powered (D). Customize your build by adding or removing rail.

6. The cart rides the rail to a detector rail that activates the redstone ladder. The signal burst up the ladder starts the redstone clock on top of the platform. The dispenser filled with arrows at the end of the redstone clock starts firing at the wooden button (E). Check out Lab 7 (page 50) for directions on how to build a redstone ladder.

7. The last step is for the minecart with pumpkin pie in the chest to be delivered to the original firing station. The arrows from the dispenser activate the redstone rail and send the cart on its way.

NOW TRY THIS

Search for Rube Goldberg in the app store on your mobile device for more Rube Goldberg machine fun.

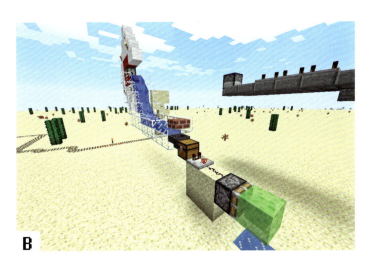

B

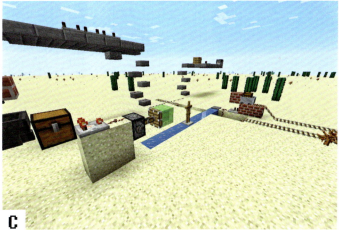

C

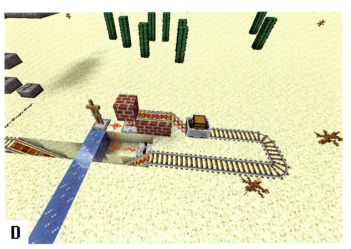

D

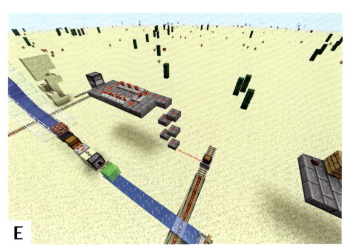

E

Pocket Solar System

You'll be diving into astronomy in this lab, where the challenge is to make a mini solar system in Minecraft. You'll park the planets in the sky right outside your science lab and create a beautiful nighttime view. In the family activity, you will focus on the ringed planet Saturn and make a clay model of its interior.

WHAT'S THE SCIENCE?

Planets in the inner solar system are solid, with heavy metallic cores. In the early solar system, the intense heat vaporized gases like hydrogen and helium and left these planets with hard, rocky surfaces. Saturn, like the other three outer planets, is known as a gas giant. The early outer solar system was much cooler. Common gases like helium and hydrogen did not vaporize and, instead, formed large gas planets with super-hot cores.

👥 FAMILY ACTIVITY
Clay Saturn

In this lab, you will be creating a model of the planet Saturn out of clay.

⏳ APPROXIMATE TIME TO COMPLETE
1 hour

✂ MATERIALS
+ 5 blocks of modeling clay, about 4 ounces (113 g) each, in assorted colors
+ Rolling pin
+ 10 toothpicks
+ Sharp knife (get help from an adult)

1. Although Saturn is a gas planet, astronomers think its core may be solid. Roll half a block of clay into a ball (A). We used black clay to form the solid core.

2. Select another color of clay and roll about half of it out flat. Cover the core with this "liquid neon" layer (B). Repeat to add two more layers, helium and hydrogen (C, D). Helium is pink and hydrogen is yellow in our model.

3. To create the ring disk, roll out the final color into a flat circle. With a toothpick, cut a hole out of the center that's just slightly smaller than your planet (E). Insert the toothpicks around the equator (F) to support the ring disk, then lay the ring disk on top of the toothpicks, stretching the center as needed.

4. With a sharp knife and adult supervision, cut a quarter section out of the planet to expose its interior (G).

A

B

C

D

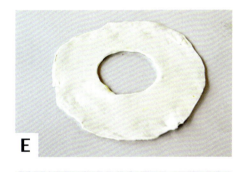

E

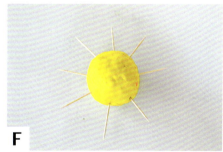

F

G

Design and Build a Solar System

Gather the family and a few friends to help you create a solar system. In this lab, you'll use math to construct planetoids to enhance the sky view from your laboratory.

1. To build in the sky, you'll need to make a tall pillar that extends high into the air. Where you stop will be the base (or south pole) of your first planet. You likely already know about a number line. You might even have experience with graphing numbers using the coordinate system. It's the same system used in Minecraft to determine your location: x, y, and z.

2. Circles and spheres have a radius, which is the distance from the center to the outer edge. We'll make our first sphere with a radius of five. Remember that number; it will come up again. Place your first block on the base (south pole of your planet) and then ten more straight up for a total of eleven blocks. This will be the y-axis. Find the center and add five blocks on both sides. This is the x-axis. Finally, repeat this step from the center to create the z-axis (A).

3. At the end of each axis, create an X reaching outward from each end block by adding two blocks in all directions (B). We used green wool. Fill in each X to create a 5 × 5 square, but leave out each corner (C).

GAME MODE
Creative

⧗ APPROXIMATE TIME TO COMPLETE
1–2 hours

FIND IT ONLINE
Want to create even more amazing shapes? Look no further than the Plotz website, a handy tool that helps you visualize Minecraft structures in 3D: *plotz.co.uk*.

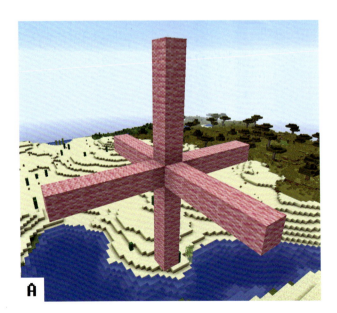

A

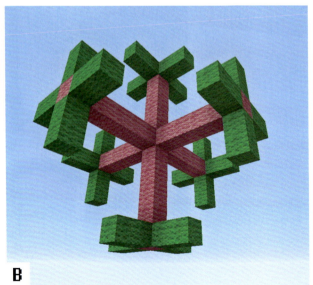

B

4. Beginning at the bottom, add two rows of five blocks each that climb like stairs upward. We used blue wool. Repeat this step from the top downward (D).

5. Complete a similar task to step 3, but instead of rows, create two columns of five blocks (yellow wool in image). Add these columns all the way around the sphere (E).

6. Finally, add a few more blocks to fill in the remaining gaps and you'll end up with your first planet (F)! We used orange wool.

7. Repeat this process and create as many planets as you would like. Experiment with different blocks, colors, and textures to create the ultimate solar system.

NOW TRY THIS

+ Construct a larger planet with a radius of seven or nine. Is there a relationship between the radius and the number of rows and columns?

+ Add a ring around a planet. Your ring should be at least three times the radius of the planet.

+ Create a star like our Sun by using glowstone.

C

D

E

F

Under the Sea

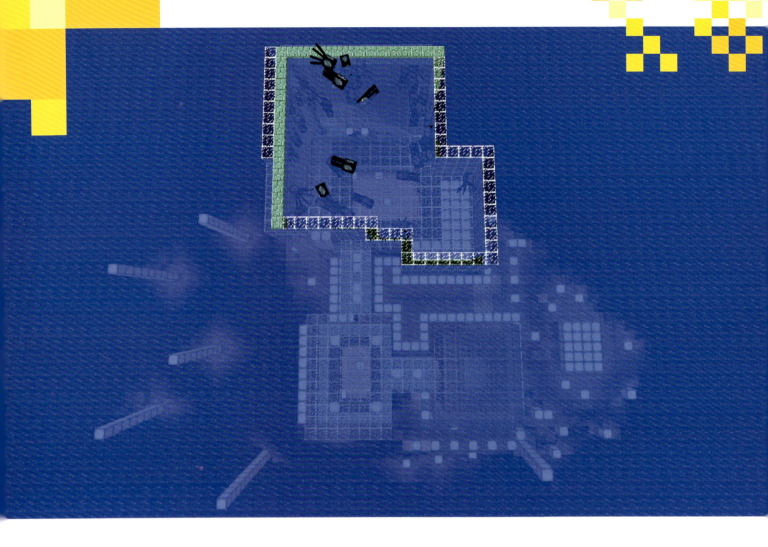

Put on your scuba gear! We're going to dive deep under the ocean and build an underwater oceanography station, a structure that will keep you safe, well fed, and investigating the bottom of the sea for hours. To begin, let's make a submarine and learn about the science of buoyancy.

This activity requires adult supervision and participation. You'll make a submarine out of plastic bottles (a great opportunity to recycle some empties), sink it, and then use your lung power to raise it once again.

WHAT'S THE SCIENCE?

In terms a scientist would use, when the upward force of buoyancy is equal to the downward force of gravity, an object floats. To sink (submerge) your submarine, you let water into the outside tanks through the large hole in each, then gravity took over. To raise your submarine, you forced air into the tanks through the straw, forcing the water out. The upward force overcame the downward force.

Bathtub Submarine

⧗ APPROXIMATE TIME TO COMPLETE
30 minutes

✂ MATERIALS
+ Small plastic or paper funnel
+ 1 large (2L) plastic bottle
+ Sand, enough to fill most of the large bottle
+ Scissors
+ 2 smaller (12 oz, 355 ml) plastic bottles
+ 4 rubber bands
+ 2 drinking straws
+ Small amount of nonhardening modeling clay
+ 2 binder clips
+ Ruler
+ Aquarium, water tank, or bathtub with water, and large enough to contain your model submarine

1. Gather your materials. Using a funnel, fill the large plastic bottle with enough sand so that it gently sinks in the water. In our example, we filled the bottle two-thirds full (A).

2. With the scissors, poke a small hole in one side of the first small bottle. The hole needs to be large enough for a straw to enter. Find the opposite side of the small bottle and poke a larger hole, about twice the size of the first hole. Repeat with the second smaller bottle (B).

3. Attach the small bottles (buoyancy tanks) on either side of the large bottle using the rubber bands. The small hole for each straw should be on top. Insert a straw into the hole in the top of each small bottle. Smear modeling clay around each straw to create a watertight seal. Attach a binder clip at the midpoint on each straw. This will be used to trap the air supply in each tank (C).

4. Place your submarine into the water. It should float as each buoyancy tank contains enough trapped gas to equalize forces. Release each binder clip. The gas trapped inside each tank will escape through the straw and water will enter the larger hole underneath. The forces are no longer equal and your sub sinks.

5. Now try to raise it from the bottom. Blow into both straws at the same time to force the water out and the carbon dioxide back into each tank. The submarine will rise as each tank fills with the less dense gas.

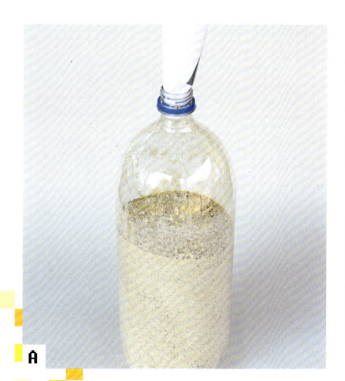

A

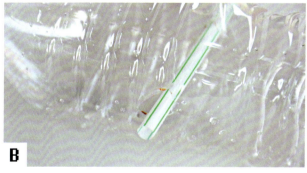

B

C

Oceanography Station

Your challenge is to take what you've learned in this book and apply it to an underwater oceanography field station. You'll need your automation skills, command block knowledge, and a solid understanding of redstone mechanisms to make it work.

Lay out your field station on paper, first. It should include the following:

- Access to food and shelter
- A power supply
- Automated doors or a mob trap
- A teleport station to return to the surface hub
- A large fish tank and viewing platform

1. Working underwater can be a difficult challenge. You can't see very well, you move more slowly, and you need to remove lots of water as you build. Find a location that isn't too deep and is mostly flat. Lay out a large number of glowstone or sea lantern blocks to light your work area (A).

2. To get the hang of building underwater, let's start with a small section of your field station. In our model, we started with the bedroom that has the dimensions of 6 × 7. Lay down the floor and put up the walls and the roof. Place a door. The door creates an air pocket, even if it is left open. With the door closed, place a sponge in your hand and right-click. The sponge will absorb all the water in the room, leaving you with a wet sponge and a dry bedroom (B).

3. As you complete each building, surround it with a layer of glass, clear or colored. Now you can punch out windows anywhere without being flooded and it stops water drops from leaking through your roofed areas (C).

GAME MODE
Creative

⏳ APPROXIMATE TIME TO COMPLETE
3–4 hours

GO BEYOND

Dive into one of the world's great aquariums, Monterey Bay Aquarium, in Monterey, California. View online exhibits and fun activities: *bit.ly/3zCCKTp*.

A

B

4. Connect separate builds with long corridors. Use lots of light and glass. Soak up the water as described in step 2 (D).

5. Build a room that has a great view of the ocean beyond and turn it into a giant aquarium by surrounding it with glass walls, several blocks away from your building (E). Place items on the sea floor that might be found in an aquarium and spawn squid when finished.

6. Finish by adding a teleport station, redstone-powered piston doors, and a power supply (F). Add as many extras as you need to complete the challenge. You'll need a way back to land.

FIND IT ONLINE

Looking for some truly crazy things to incorporate into you undersea lab? Check out UnspeakableGaming's twenty-minute video full of redstone ideas: *bit.ly/3S62b5Q*.

NOW TRY THIS

+ How else could you use command blocks in this build? Experiment with the /summon command in your aquarium.

+ Every oceanographer needs a submarine. Build one and attach it to the lab by creating a docking station.

C

D

E

F

Extras

Scavenger Hunt Checklist

- ☐ Apple
- ☐ Bed
- ☐ Boat
- ☐ Bow and arrow
- ☐ Bread
- ☐ Cactus
- ☐ Cake
- ☐ Carpet
- ☐ Carrot
- ☐ Clay
- ☐ Coal or charcoal
- ☐ Cobweb
- ☐ Compass
- ☐ Diamond
- ☐ Dirt
- ☐ Egg
- ☐ Emerald
- ☐ Fish
- ☐ Fishing rod

- ☐ Flower pot
- ☐ Flowers
- ☐ Furnace
- ☐ Glass
- ☐ Gold
- ☐ Grass
- ☐ Gravel
- ☐ Hoe
- ☐ Ice or snow
- ☐ Iron
- ☐ Ladder
- ☐ Leather
- ☐ Leaves
- ☐ Melon
- ☐ Milk
- ☐ Music disc
- ☐ Obsidian
- ☐ Painting
- ☐ Pickaxe

- ☐ Pumpkin pie
- ☐ Saddle
- ☐ Sand
- ☐ Shovel
- ☐ Sign
- ☐ Spider eye
- ☐ Sponge
- ☐ Stairs
- ☐ Sticks
- ☐ Stone
- ☐ String
- ☐ Sugar
- ☐ Tree
- ☐ Vines
- ☐ Water bottle
- ☐ Water bucket
- ☐ Wheat
- ☐ Wood plank
- ☐ Wool

Shadow Puppet Pattern

Butterfly pattern for Lab 12 Setting the Stage (see page 70).

Dot Programming Sheet

Dot programming sheet for Lab 21 Code Your Commands (see page 114).

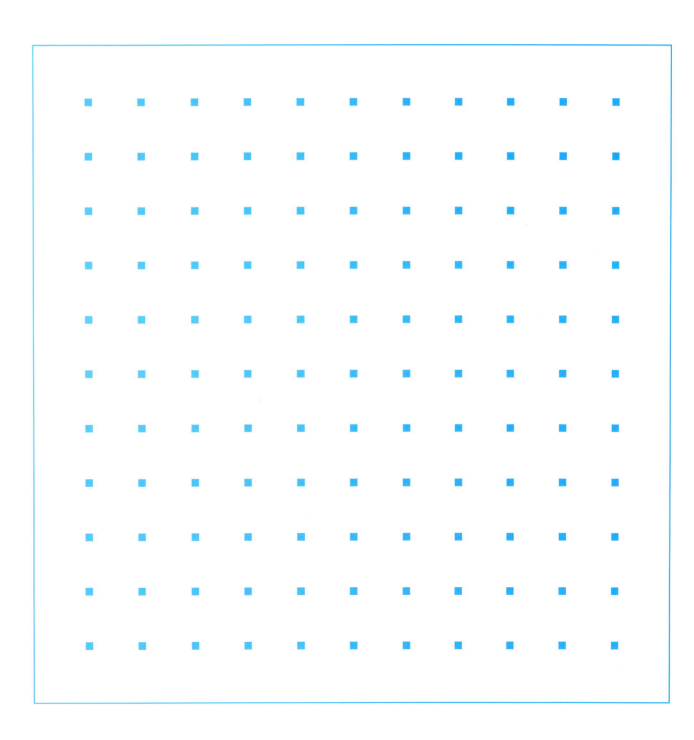

LAB NUMBER AND TITLE	FEATURED STEM CONCEPT(S)	NGSS (Next Generation Science Standards) www.nextgenscience.org	INTERNATIONAL BACCALAUREATE www.ibo.org
1 Do You Mine?	Geology, chemistry, problem-solving	Constructing explanations; Material properties	Learner agency
2 It's Electric!	Energy transfer, circuits, engineering design	Energy; Force; Cause and effect	Physics: Energy, circuits. Math: Patterns, functions, modeling
3 Setting a Trap	Gravity, water flow, engineering	Developing and using models; Designing solutions	Approaches to learning; Simple experiment
4 Fire When Ready!	Force and motion, potential and kinetic energy, simple machines	Planning and carrying out investigations; Constructing explanations and designing solutions; Motions and forces; Energy	Approaches to learning; Developing key concepts; Experimental sciences
5 Redstone Laboratory	Electrical engineering, photovoltaic sensors, solar astronomy, programming, note and pitch	Motion and Stability: Forces and Interactions	Physics: Stellar Quantities, Energy Sources
6 All Aboard	Inertia, kinetic and potential energy, velocity	Motion and Stability: Forces and Interactions	Physics: Work, Energy and Power, Momentum and Impulse
7 Gravity Impact	Kinetic energy, energy transference	Earth's Systems	Physics: Work, Energy and Power, Newton's Law of Gravitation
8 Piston Power	Pascal's principle, density and pressure	Matter and Its Interactions	Physics: Fluid and Fluid Dynamics
9 Grow a Garden	Plant growth and development, ecosystems, environmental factors	Molecules and Organisms: Structures and Processes; Ecosystems: Interactions, energy, and dynamics	Biology (plant biology, ecosystems); Chemistry (soil chemistry); Physics (light and energy)
10 Flying Machine	Mechanics, physics, engineering design	Motion and Stability: Forces and Interactions; Engineering Design	Sciences: Physics (forces, motion); Mathematics (geometry, measurement)
11 Creating Figures	Spatial reasoning, scale and proportion	Planning and carrying out investigations; Constructing explanations and designing solutions	Transdisciplinary themes; Approaches to learning; Problem-solving

LAB NUMBER AND TITLE	FEATURED STEM CONCEPT(S)	NGSS (Next Generation Science Standards) www.nextgenscience.org	INTERNATIONAL BACCALAUREATE www.ibo.org
12 Setting the Stage	Social sciences and storytelling integration, communication and collaboration	Constructing explanations and designing solutions	Transdisciplinary themes; Developing key concepts; Creativity, communication, and collaboration
13 Map Maker	Geography and technology	Earth's Systems	Individuals and Societies
14 Let There Be Light	Exothermic and endothermic reactions, chemistry, electromagnetic spectrum	Waves and Electromagnetic Radiation	Physics: Momentum and Impulse; Chemistry: Entropy and Spontaneity
15 Crystals	Thermal energy, exothermic reactions	Earth's Systems	Physics: Thermal Concepts
16 Catch a Wave	Wave Energy	Waves and Their Applications in Technologies for Information Transfer	Physics: Traveling Waves, Wave Characteristics, Wave Behavior
17 Egg Farm	Agriculture, engineering, programming	Earth and Human Activity	Biology: Classification of Biodiversity
18 Build a Battery	Chemical energy, electrical energy	Energy	Physics: Electric Cells
19 Create an Ecosystem	Horticulture	Ecosystems: Interactions, Energy, and Dynamics	Physics: Thermal Concepts; Biology: Water, Nutrient Cycling
20 Quantum Physics	Polarization, coding	Waves and Their Applications in Technologies for Information Transfer	Physics: Quantum and Nuclear Physics
21 Code Your Commands	Technology, coding	ISTE student standards	ISTE student standards
22 Chain Reaction Contraption	Simple machines	Motion and Stability: Forces and Interactions	Physics: Forces
23 Pocket Solar System	Astronomy, geology, geometry	Space Systems	Physics: Measurements in Physics, Stellar Quantities
24 Under the Sea	Buoyancy, ecosystem	Ecosystems: Interactions, Energy, and Dynamics	Biology: Species and Communities, Communities and Ecosystems

3D Printing
printcraft.org

Adam Clarke
thecommonpeople.tv

Adobe Captivate
adobe.com/products/captivate.html

Anaglyphs of Mars
go.nasa.gov/3SscNfT

Blockworks
blockworksmc.com

Camtasia
techsmith.com/camtasia.html

Color Vision
bit.ly/3ycTpwp

Command Block
bit.ly/4dDoLLR

Commands
bit.ly/46mneag

Commands and Cheats
bit.ly/4foYKBg

Cooked Chicken Farm
bit.ly/3WknnI8

Coordinates of a Block
bit.ly/4cQcgMY

Creative Commons Music
*creativecommons.org/
legalmusicforvideos*

Crystals in Mineral Water
bit.ly/4d24HCt

**Games and Activities:
Monterey Bay Aquarium**
bit.ly/3zCCKTp

**Jesper the End's Minecraft
Disco Party**
bit.ly/3Y2Q3GN

John Miller's Blog
johnmilleredu.com

Kundt's tube
bit.ly/46k8Lfg

**Making of When
Stampy Came to Tea**
bit.ly/4czYygQ

Marble Roller Coaster
bit.ly/4cXuxHB

Minecraft Shapes
plotz.co.uk

Note Block
bit.ly/3zCBQ9k

Pixel Papercraft
pixelpapercraft.com

Rainbow Beacon
bit.ly/4bGvZND

Redstone Creations
bit.ly/3Lm0RIr

Redstone Doors and Trapdoors
bit.ly/3S9v7dl

Redstone Tutorials
bit.ly/3zBB2l3

Rube Goldberg
rubegoldberg.org

Science Friday
bit.ly/3A3ufAY

ScreenPal
bit.ly/3LHk7jI

Shadow Puppets
bit.ly/3W4NIIG

**Slicedlime—Learn Minecraft
Commands**
bit.ly/46dlUGW

Terraria
terraria.org

**Traps, Advanced Building
Techniques**
bit.ly/3zFtIF2

Underwater Redstone House
bit.ly/4f3Yk3p

Vacuum Chamber by BBC
bit.ly/3xSOHDU

When Stampy Came to Tea
bit.ly/4czXtpi

Working Dam
bit.ly/3WiYMDp

YouTube Editor
youtube.com/editor

Zombie Party YouTube Playlist
bit.ly/3W4hflK

I would like to acknowledge the support, hard work, and dedication of my wife, Audrey, in the completion of this book.
—JM

I want to express my deepest gratitude to my wonderful wife, Annie. Thank you for being my biggest cheerleader and for always inspiring me to follow my passions.
—CFS

About the Authors

JOHN MILLER is an instructional coach and retired middle school science and history teacher with thirty years' experience. He holds a master's degree in educational technology and instructional design from San Diego State University. He has been recognized as a Google Innovator, Microsoft curriculum developer, Minecraft Education lesson designer, and finalist for California Teacher of the Year. In 2017, John was granted a Fulbright Teaching Award, which provided an opportunity for him to work with the Ministry of Education in Singapore to explore the effectiveness of game-based learning in the classroom.

CHRIS FORNELL SCOTT is the Executive Director of Woven Learning and Technology, a 501(c)(3) nonprofit that delivers engaging, hands-on workshops for underserved youth. Passionate about empowering young minds, Chris is dedicated to inspiring a love for learning and providing opportunities for children from diverse backgrounds.

Outside of his professional role, Chris is a proud father of three teenage boys and a loving husband. He loves the ocean and is always eager to learn new things, continually seeking ways to grow and expand his horizons.

Index

Quarto.com

© 2025 Quarto Publishing Group USA Inc.
Text © 2016, 2018 Quarto Publishing Group USA Inc.

First Published in 2024 by Quarry Books, an imprint of The Quarto Group,
100 Cummings Center, Suite 265-D, Beverly, MA 01915, USA.
T (978) 282-9590 F (978) 283-2742

Quarry Books titles are also available at discount for retail, wholesale, promotional, and bulk purchase. For details, contact the Special Sales Manager by email at specialsales@quarto.com or by mail at The Quarto Group, Attn: Special Sales Manager, 100 Cummings Center, Suite 265-D, Beverly, MA 01915, USA.

NOT AN OFFICIAL MINECRAFT PRODUCT. NOT APPROVED BY OR ASSOCIATED WITH MOJANG OR MICROSOFT

10 9 8 7 6 5 4 3 2 1

ISBN: 978-0-7603-9623-0

Digital edition published in 2025
eISBN: 978-0-7603-9624-7

Library of Congress Cataloging-in-Publication Data available
The content in this book was previously published in *Unofficial Minecraft Lab for Kids* (Quarry Books 2016) and *Unofficial Minecraft STEM Lab for Kids* (Quarry Books 2018) both by John Miller and Chris Fornell Scott.

Design and Page Layout: Mattie Wells Design
Cover Image: Adobe Stock
Photography: John Miller and Chris Fornell Scott, except: Glenn Scott Photography on page 4, 7, 10, 11, 14, 67, 71; Shutterstock.com on page 21 and 59; GTS Productions on page 63, and biblphoto on page 135.

Printed in China